Era of Undying

The Ichorian Epics: Book One

Emilie Knight

Illustration and Design: David Schmelling

Printed in Canada

First Printing, 2017

ISBN: 978-1979094320

Prologue

The night was warm, though clouds hung heavily, obscuring the moonlight over the countryside of Ichorisis. The pleasant weather made the small caravan of travelers settle down early by the fire. There were maybe a dozen people in the caravan, so one could easily assume they were just a family of merchants. One aspect that contradicted that idea was how little the group was carrying. Pen had been watching them long enough to know that once anything of value came into their hands, it was quickly sold or hidden away. She had been following them for a while and learned that they hid the most valuables items in a small lock box tied to the leader's horse.

The leader of the caravan was close to the fire, carving into a boar. His arms were painted crimson past his elbows. Everyone else was strewn about doing various tasks, but most of them were sitting lazily by the fire, listening to a short man with scar tissue covering his left arm tell a hunting story. Soon afterwards when the boar was cooked, they all ate and talked and laughed. When most of the boar was gone they settled down for sleep leaving the half eaten carcass over the coals. The leader had eaten with gore still on his hands but had washed up in the nearby creek before using a saddlebag as a pillow. Two of them stayed awake to keep watch. One stayed by the horses, while the other walked around their makeshift perimeter. Neither saw Pen crouched behind the thorn bush.

Silently, she crept out from the bush to follow the man behind the tree line. He kept the caravan in sight but wandered a good distance into the trees. She wondered what he was doing; he wasn't patrolling. He walked aimlessly, then stopped. She heard running water then realized he was relieving himself. He was clearly relaxed and sensed no danger. She picked up a rock and threw it. It *thunked* against a tree and fell into a bush. The man glanced toward the rustling noise but dismissed it. She almost felt bad at how easy this would be. Then her stomach growled. Gritting her teeth and clenching her stomach muscles, she stifled the noise, but her nerve wavered. Her last proper meal had been three days ago. Doing her best to ignore the hunger pains, she gripped her knife. As the man was arranging his trousers, she stood behind him and struck.

One of Pen's hands covered his mouth first, catching him off guard. He grunted in surprise, but the blade across his throat silenced him quickly. He panicked and buckled as his life pulsed from his throat, but she kept her hold. He was heavy, but she managed to ease him to the ground in near silence. No one moved in the camp, and no one heard their friend die. It took a moment for the blood to finish flowing out, and she cringed when he coughed more over her hand. It wasn't the first time she'd felt that much blood, of course, and it was by no means the last; it had to be done. She wiped her hand and knife on the dead man's woolen tunic, then turned back to the shadows.

Keeping low, avoiding the dry twigs, she made it around the camp to where the horses were tethered. The other man was leaning against a tree, flask in hand. He was closer to the camp, so she couldn't kill him without exposing herself or spooking the horses. She didn't want to risk sneaking closer to the horses and the strongbox, he was beside the leader's horse. She hid behind a thick oak tree and searched around for a dry stick on the ground. She stepped down hard. It made a crisp *snap* in the silence.

The man looked up and gazed into the darkness in her direction. Pen darted from one tree to another and crouched under the pine branches. He saw her. Stepping away from his tree, he peered into the forest and came closer. He glanced at his companions, then back at the trees. He put the flask away and unsheathed his sword silently, presumably so as not to alarm the others, and then approached her hiding place. He passed her, then paused. Her heart was in her throat. She prayed he wouldn't shout.

"Who's there?" he called.

It wasn't enough to wake the camp, thankfully. The man grumbled "rabbit", sheathed his sword, and turned back. He passed her again, and she slipped out of hiding to stand behind him. She must be quick and silent: she stabbed the knife into his ear. She used too much force, though, and he hit a maple tree while falling, rattling the branches. He was dead, at least.

She took a breath, forcing her heart rate to slow. She saw no sign of anyone stirring in the camp, so she approached the horses again. The leader of the caravan might have been sleeping on his saddlebags, but the lockbox was attached directly to the horse's saddle, hidden under leather. He probably thought it was safer because it was unexpected. The lockbox was strapped to the saddle, with two locks on the straps themselves. Luckily, the dozing horse provided a little cover, but Pen was still within the ring of firelight, and her legs were exposed. She took out her lock picking pins and went to work. The second lock gave her a harder time, but both clicked open. The lid of the small box squeaked, but no one noticed. Inside was a silver pendant with a ruby on a thin chain, and a gold ring. Their price could buy her food for at least a week.

A twig snapped behind her.

She spun with knife in hand, but pain erupted in her head and everything went black.

She was on the ground when she came to with a splitting headache. Panic grabbed hold of her when she realized she couldn't move. Her hands were tied behind her back, and her feet were bound too. The panic nearly won when she realized she was by the fire, with the entire camp surrounding her.

"I'll admit I didn't take you for a woman at first."

The leader stood over her with his arms crossed. He was a big man with thick black hair and beard.

She shifted to her knees, which was awkward with her hands tied, but she managed. Her vision was blurred from the blow, but it was clearing. There were eleven men and women standing around her, three of them behind her, and one small figure sitting by a tree behind the leader.

"You even killed two of my best fighters," the leader said casually, as though this were an everyday conversation.

"Even the best can get lazy and ignore the shadows." She couldn't feel warmth spreading from where she was struck so she didn't think she was bleeding; there would probably be a good bruise later. She started twisting her wrist into the rope.

"Let's just kill her. She murdered Belos!" said a skinny man holding a bow.

"And Hason," a woman added.

The rest of the followers muttered in agreement.

The leader raised a hand and they stopped grumbling.

"Not until we've had a little chat," the leader said. He knelt before Pen. "Did anyone send you?" His voice made her want to shiver despite the fire's warmth.

She looked him directly in the eye. "No."

"Are you alone?"

"No," she lied. She wasn't sure if he believed her. He had a good face for gambling.

"What are you doing with your arm?" He sounded intrigued but not entirely distracted.

"Escaping."

He laughed.

She felt her wrist sting, then blood trickled down her hand.

He chuckled and stood. "I honestly don't know if I want to kill you or let you join us."

"She murdered Belos!" the skinny man yelled again.

"I know he was your brother, and I will mourn him too." His steely voice made the other man look away. "She struck silently, and that could be useful. But considering I don't let anyone already in kill a member without due punishment, I can't just let in someone who did kill a member. Killing her would be safer and easier."

"She's pretty, though, sir," a burly man said. "Can we play with her first?"

"Normally I wouldn't care, but she's proven to be an efficient assassin. I don't think—"

She willed her blood to rise. Sensing there the three stood behind her she shot her blood toward them, striking two in the throat and one in the eye. At the same moment she hardened it into a blade to cut the ropes. As the first three fell gurgling and screaming, she stood to face the others, snaking the strings of blood around so it floated in front of her.

All of her opponents had drawn their weapons, but now they froze. Three tendrils of solid blood floated several feet from her wrist, sharpened to points facing the bandits.

Staying calm was a challenge, but she managed it. Panic would cloud her thoughts and thin her blood.

"I don't believe it," one man muttered.

"M'lady," the leader said. One of his hands held an axe, but he raised the other to show peace. "No one else needs to die tonight. You can walk away, and no one here will repeat what happened."

"Rumors spread like wildfire," Pen replied.

"Not this one. You can keep what was in the lockbox, plus anything else I have of value. You can take what you need and go."

"The hell she will!" the skinny man shouted.

He fired an arrow at Pen's heart.

One tendril caught the arrow, twisted it around, and stuck it into his neck. Three more men charged her with swords in hand. Two were pierced through the heart, but the last one was too close. Pen retracted the tendrils and dived under his blade, which was aimed at her head. She changed her blood into a blade and stuck him in the gut. He fell groaning while she stood with a crimson blade in hand.

One woman charged at her with a hammer. Pen killed her with a dodge then a slice to the neck, following through to the next man, lopping off his arm before stabbing him in the chest. Another turned to run, but she extended her sword into a spear and got him in the back. That left the leader, who had stayed back until now. She faced him.

He had his axe at the ready. She considered switching to a sword for speed but kept the spear for distance.

"Damn that Hados, he was always a wild card," he growled. "You're the Blood Warrior."

She stayed quiet.

"If you leave me be, I'll tell no one of this."

"I can't do that." She didn't enjoy killing, but it was necessary. No one could know she existed. Not after what happened to the last Warriors.

"Fine, then." He had no intention of dying.

He stalked to the left. She followed, stepping over a body. He lunged with the axe, but she parried with the spear. His fist flew, catching the side of her face.

Stunned, she staggered back but managed to avoid his next swing. She caught his axe with her spear and pulled him off balance, hitting him over the head with the end of it. Then she melted her spear, changed it into a hammer, and brought it down on the back of his head.

He went down hard but caught himself on his knees. She sharpened her hammer into an axe and embedded it in his skull.

She slumped among the bodies next to the fire, panting, and listened for any movement, tense with anticipation of another attack, but none came. Then she remembered the small figure by the tree. She stood and saw a boy, perhaps ten years old, hiding behind the tree. He was staring at her and trembling.

The boy bolted into the forest. She swore and followed him. The chase only lasted a few minutes before she lost him in the gloom. She cursed louder. The boy would tell people what he saw. Rumors of her existence would spread. Cursing again, she went back to the dead camp.

She cleaned any dirt or blood that was not her own off her axe. Once it was clean, it lost its form and melted back into her wrist. Despondent, she sat by the fire and ate her fill of what was left of the boar. There wasn't much after having been picked over by a dozen people. At least her stomach was full for one more night. She then took a pack and filled it with what food was left, along with the valuables the traveling bandits had hidden on them as well the jewelry from the lockbox.

She took the saddles off all of the horses except the leader's. It looked the strongest; a big gray and black speckled stallion. Hefting the new pack and mounting her new horse, she rode off.

Chapter One

The day was cheery enough. Clouds filled the sky, casting gray over the marketplace, but it was relatively warm for the ninth moon of the year. The city of Stymphalia was lively, and the western market was crowded with merchants, fishmongers, blacksmiths, and a very large number of people. Pen stood uncomfortably at the edge of the crowd. She swallowed her nerves, since there was no way to avoid them all.

The cobbler's shop was almost empty, which was a blessing. There was only one other patron, who left shortly after Pen entered. The cobbler, who had light blue hair, fixed his attention on her.

"And how might you be today, m'lord?"

She pushed back her hood, revealing dark purple hair that hung to her shoulders.

"My lady," the cobbler corrected himself quickly. "My apologies."

"It's alright. I need new boots. Preferably tall ones to survive the mud." A hole had finally been worn through the side of her current pair.

"Boots, m'lady? Are you sure you wouldn't prefer a pair of sandals or slippers? In fact, I've just finished a pair of sandals that tie all the way up the leg."

"Boots are fine." Pen began playing with two coppers from her purse.

"Very well." He led her to one side of the shop, having seen that she could pay well for his work; a pair was only worth one copper.

It took some time to find a good pair. Pen wasn't particular about style, but she wanted to be comfortable, and most of these boots were too big. She paid the cobbler two coppers and walked out with simple black leather boots.

Pen stopped at a stand and bought a meat pie from a small girl and her mother. The pie was good, but she couldn't place the taste of the meat. It could have been cat. The pie brought up the memory of her son Alard, who had always enjoyed the pies she had made. Her husband Arch loved them too, when they could afford the beef. She'd never thought of making one from a cat, Alard liked cats as a pet: she couldn't make him eat one. The taste of the pie died in her mouth at the thought of her family. She missed them. Her throat tightened at the thought of their deaths.

"—looked terrified."

Pen had perched on top of a low wall to eat her pie when a voice caught her ear. Taking a quick, casual glance, she saw it came from the guard of the city watch.

"Of course he was scared. The kid saw his family killed," his companion said.

"Not just killed: slaughtered by the Blood Warrior. I was there in the Hall, heard him with my own ears."

The pie didn't taste very good any more.

"The kid was scared, so of course the facts were vague," his friend said. "Besides, it's just a kid with an imagination, a traumatic event, and a rumor that crops up every year or so."

"Still, those rumors have done more than crop up. What about that inn? There must have been at least twenty men in there."

"I heard it was a savage with an axe from the mountains, but I also heard it was three travelers from across the river. Even heard it was a witch with a pointy hat." His voice had become mocking.

"I get it, probably nothing."

"Although, I am impressed by the man who survived the spear through the chest in that inn."

"I heard someone survived falling off the west guard tower yesterday."

"He was definitely a lucky, drunk fool."

Pen forced down the morsel in her mouth and threw the rest of the pie to a stray dog. The guards had left a bitter taste in her mouth despite the pie. She knew the attack of which they spoke. The boy with those bandits had escaped, and she had let him. She could have tracked him down but chose not to. Finding him would have been the only way to ensure his silence, but that would have meant killing him. Pen knew rumors were spreading, they always did, but she had had no idea the boy had been heading for the capital! Leaving now was the best idea, but it was dusk, which was when the city closed its gates for the night. She hoped luck was on her side.

It wasn't. Standing at the corner of the street, watching the cold iron gates close, Pen considered sneaking out, but she didn't want to stir up any trouble or draw attention. She turned on her heel and walked to the nearest inn, not wanting to go back to the one she'd used last night lest someone recognize her.

This inn was larger than the last one, with three floors. The traffic in the area must contribute to its patronage. With the last of her spoils from the road bandits Pen paid for a flagon, some cooked chicken, and a room. She took her food to the corner of the tavern, beside the unlit fireplace. With her back to the wall, she ate and listened.

There was the usual chatter of people complaining about taxes and about other people, or swapping stories of war and spoils. The tavern was large and it was darkening with the setting sun. The innkeeper came out of the kitchen and lit the fire, brightening the room again. The shadows were pushed back and twitched along the walls. The smell of smoke filled the air, mixing with the chicken and too many unwashed bodies.

A group close by caught her attention. They were talking about the king collapsing in court today. She felt like she should be worried, like everyone else, but although she had been born in this land, the people were never part of her home. She hardly cared about the royal family; people were necessary to life, of course, like the cobbler, but she paid them no mind and they left her alone. She preferred it that way, but there were exceptions, of course, like the road bandits. Once her chicken was finished and the flagon empty, she went upstairs to sleep. She had lucked out with the bed this time; there were no bugs.

Pen woke the next morning with rain pounding on the window. That was good: it would cover her tracks as she left. Breakfast was a thick porridge that she heard the innkeeper priding himself on. Pen thought it was rather bland.

A man entered the inn, judging by his armour, he was another member of the city guard. He probably wanted some of that bland porridge before starting his rounds. Pen allowed herself one look at the guard to note his position in the room, but her glance became a stare. The boy from the road bandits' camp was with him. The guard was probably taking him to an orphanage after breaking his fast.

Pen pulled up her hood, pretending to be cold, and kept her face down, forcing herself to eat at a normal pace. She tried not to think about how dead the boy's eyes looked, but failed. The room was calm, with most of the patrons most likely nursing headaches from the night before, based on the commotion she'd heard from her room.

"Oi, bard." A man tossed a youth by the fire a coin. "Play something cheerful."

"Anything in particular?" the bard asked.

"Nah, just something to wake up to."

The bard tuned his lute and began a song about a girl and her knight.

Pen gulped down the rest of her breakfast. The bard was seated behind her, and the boy was watching him.

"That's her!"

The bard stopped singing. All chatter died. Pen sensed the boy pointing at her before she looked up. The entire inn had turned to face her. None looked friendly, but most were just confused by the interruption.

"What?" Pen acted just as confused. Her heart thudded in her ears, but she managed to maintain an appearance of calm.

"It was you that killed them. You killed my father!" the boy shouted "You made your blood move."

The entire room was still with rising tension. The guard loosened the sword at his belt.

"What?" Pen scoffed, playing dumb. "I understand you must be grieving, but don't accuse the first person you see, boy."

She stood to leave. Luckily, she had brought her pack downstairs with her.

"Hold on." The guard blocked her path to the door. His hair was purple, like her own, but lighter. The stubble matched. "Murder is a heavy accusation to walk away from."

"What do you suggest I do then? My husband is waiting for me in the next city," Pen lied. "Besides the boy is wrong."

"We'll send word to your husband and bring him in as a character witness, but you're coming with me."

The entire tavern was watching, but she could only feel the accusation in the boy's eyes. He was shaking, filled with hate. Her heart went to him; no one that young should hold so much pain. The irony that she had been the one to cause it was not lost on her.

"Fine." There was no easy way to escape from here yet, anyway.

"Wait." The man who had tossed the coin to the bard stood. "Son, you said she did something with her blood?"

Damn! Pen had thought that the boy's comment had slipped by.

"She did, she made it fly around and kill everyone, and it turned into weapons."

Half of the crowd snickered. One man outright laughed, and Pen joined them, hating herself for it.

"Would that I could do that! I would be out of here in a heartbeat."

"But you did!" the boy screamed.

"A woman has never been the Blood Warrior," the man who laughed exclaimed.

"Who's to say I couldn't be a warrior?" Pen challenged. She could hold her own, even without her magic. She was slight, yes, but quick with a knife. "And what about Hamia, daughter of Maniodes? She was the first to start the bloodline."

The man scoffed. "Every true warrior is a man, after her of course. But that's just a myth anyway."

"So just because I don't have an extra piece of flesh dangling between my legs means I can't fight? I thought not having one would be advantageous, since they are so sensitive."

The man stood, clearly getting agitated. She stood her ground, one hand drifting to her knife.

The guard stepped between them. "There's no need for a fight. She's coming with me to the castle."

"Better teach her some manners while you're at it," the man growled.

The guard ushered her outside, and behind her Pen heard the chatter resume. She hoped that playing along with the blood magic accusation would divert the attention. The boy followed them.

The rain had lessened during their confrontation, but the roads were slick with mud. Once down the first street, the guard ushered over another man dressed in city watch armour. Whether he felt threatened by a single woman or the magic accusation, Pen couldn't be sure, but it was probably the magic. The boy trailed close behind as the two guards escorted her to the castle. She wanted to bolt, but that would solidify her guilt, and then she'd be wanted for sure.

The guards took her to a small room in the keep. It wasn't exactly a cell, but there were no windows. A man came in asking questions: where she was traveling to, who her husband was, which gate she had entered the city. He scribbled notes on a parchment and left without another word. More people passed along the corridor and a man was posted outside her door. She couldn't escape without causing a commotion and drawing more attention to herself. Playing along might be the safest action for now. The boy had no proof against her, but she had no proof of her innocence either. She heard the boy outside, asking the guards why they didn't just hang her.

After an hour or so another man entered. He was older, with dark green hair, and introduced himself as Tellus, captain of the city watch. They sat comfortably at the table in the centre of the room as she told him her story. Not the truth, of course, but that she was meeting her husband in the city north of the capital because he had recently acquired a new home for them.

"Through which gate did you enter the city?" he asked.

"South," she lied.

"Mm-hm. You know the kid is outside claiming your head, right?" He sounded tired.

"I can hear him, and I don't blame him for being angry. He lost his whole family." The grief in her voice was real. She hated hurting children.

"Aye, you probably got caught in the crossfire of his confusion. He just wants someone to blame."

Pen allowed herself a breath of relief; Captain Tellus was on her side.

"We've sent word to your husband, what was his name again?"

"Arch."

"Right, I read it on Connin's note. It will take some time for him to get the message, and more for him to ride down here," the captain said. "We still need to hold a trial tomorrow."

Pen's heart fell. "But you know I'm innocent."

"I believe you, but the accusation of murder still needs to be seen by the king, the blood magic even more so."

"There hasn't been a Blood Warrior for decades," Pen protested. "The last one was killed in a failed rebellion fifty years ago."

"Nonetheless, the king will be informed, and you will be put on trial." His tone broached no further argument. Pen could see why he was a captain.

There was a sudden knocking on the door. The captain seemed confused. Pen's heart rate picked up pace again at the sudden intrusion.

The captain stood and opened the door. "What is it?"

Another guard stood in the corridor. He looked nervous about interrupting his superior. "The king would like to see the woman now, sir," he said.

Pen couldn't sit still any longer. Trying to act as harmless as possible, she stood. This was not going well.

"How did he find out about her so quickly?" the captain growled.

"I believe Connin informed him, sir." The guard's voice was more sheepish now.

"Of course," the captain exclaimed. He sighed and turned to Pen. "That bastard's been a thorn in my arse for months. Come on then, lass."

She took an involuntary step back. "Now?"

"I'm afraid so. The king is waiting."

Pen didn't move. A dozen methods of escape came to mind, but all would make her seem guilty, and she would have to use her power.

"I don't have to clap you in irons and drag you there, do I?" He clearly didn't want to.

"No," Pen controlled her stammer. "I'll go."

Chapter Two

King Aegeus looked awful. Pen had heard rumors that he was sick, but she had no idea it was this bad. She was surprised he could even sit upright. His skin was the color of curdled milk, and the shadows under his eyes were as dark as bruises. He was dressed regally with a dark blue tunic and black cape, but it only made him look more worn. He held a cloth that was stained with blood, some fresh, mostly dried.

The hall was crowded with people of the court, rich nobles watching the day's proceedings for entertainment. The boy, Pen still didn't know his name, had followed Pen as the captain escorted her to the throne room. After recounting his side of the story he stood close by, fidgeting with agitation. He had painted Pen to be a ruthless murderer who killed his family by making her blood move from her hands. He was telling most of the truth, but left out that they had tied her up and were about to kill her instead. Granted, she was robbing them, but she'd had no real intentions of killing them until they saw her power, and that was the only way she could have escaped.

"You're sure this is her, boy?" King Aegeus's voice was hardly more than a croak, but it still held power.

"It is. She made her blood turn into spears and other weapons and slaughtered my family, my father!" The boy's eyes shone with tears but also triumph.

"And you say you are innocent?" King Aegeus said to Pen.

"I am, Your Grace." Pen did her best to control her nerves, but this had gotten far out of hand. "I've never met this boy until today."

"Liar!"

"Enough!" Aegeus commanded.

A fit of coughing overcame him. He pressed the cloth to his mouth as his whole body shook. The sound was muffled by the cloth, but it still sounded violent. When it passed, he took a few moments to breathe and wipe the blood from his lips.

Everyone in the hall had fallen silent to watch their king die slowly before them, like vultures waiting to strike. The king's only heir was still unborn, growing in his wife, Queen Aethra. Pen had no doubt there would be a lot of change when the king's health finally gave out.

Those vultures would be waiting a little longer, though, as King Aegeus took a shaking breath and spoke. "I'm tired of this squabbling. What do you suggest, Captain? You've heard them both, just as I have."

Pen took a breath of relief; the captain had been on her side before.

"I think we should hold her until her husband arrives, then we can have a proper trial," Captain Tellus suggested. "Your Grace."

"Yes," the king agreed. "I'd thought so too."

A voice came from the crowd. "That may not be necessary, Your Grace."

A tall man in garb similar to the captain's but lacking the badge of office stepped forward. Captain Tellus's eyebrows knitted together, and he scowled in annoyance. It was the man who had taken the notes before. Based on Tellus's expression, this must be Connin.

Connin knelt before the king. "We have a witness who saw her yesterday."

Pen's heart leapt into her throat.

"Bring him forward."

Pen had to admit that no matter how tired the king was, he got straight to business when necessary.

Connin stood and shouted, "Delmore."

A youth of no more than twenty approached the main group. Pen didn't recognize him and thought his blue hair was striking, but the stubbly beard he was trying to grow was patchy. He looked nervous to be called before the king. He couldn't make direct eye contact with the monarch for long, either, as if the sickness might spread to him.

Connin moved to stand beside Delmore. "Tell everyone what you told me."

Delmore took a moment to collect himself. Pen noted that he refused to look at her, even though his eyes were darting everywhere else. He couldn't face the woman he was condemning.

"It's nothing terribly special," he said. "I've been on duty at the North Gate, watching the local traffic for about a week now, and I saw her walk in by herself the day after last." He quickly added, "Your Grace."

Pen could hardly breathe; she scolded herself for not being more careful when entering the city. The fear was making it harder to keep still, but she disciplined herself to act calm, even confused, at his information. She had to play along, even if her instincts were telling her to run.

"You're sure it was her?" the king pressed.

"Yes, Your Grace."

"And why would you remember one face among the hundreds you must see every day?"

Delmore stammered for a moment at Aegeus's bluntness. "I had taken note of her being alone when most people arrive in groups, and—" He cut himself off.

"And?"

"And… I admired her hair," Delmore admitted.

The majority of the room snickered at the lad. He flushed and stared at the floor between his feet. Pen would have felt bad for him if he hadn't just condemned her.

King Aegeus called for silence, and the vultures stopped chuckling.

"There's nothing wrong with fancying a girl, lad," he said calmly.

Delmore kept staring at the floor. That was probably a good idea, because Pen wanted to gouge out his eyes.

King Aegeus coughed again, but this time it wasn't so violent. "Tellus, you said she came from the South Gate."

"That's what she told me, Your Grace." Tellus looked at Pen. Any sense of trust or innocence was gone.

"Well miss… what is your name again?"

"Pen."

"Right, do you have anything to say on this matter? You've been quiet for some time."

Pen prayed her nervousness wasn't making her look guilty; she was aiming to appear as an innocent maid. "He must have seen someone else. I came from the south."

"Well, someone is lying." Another coughing fit took hold. Pen couldn't help cringing; it looked like he couldn't breathe. The cloth in his hand was more red than white now.

"We… we will resume on the morrow," he said after finally gulping for air. "Tellus, take her to one of the cells and keep the boy close by."

Tellus took her by the arm and was about to lead her away, but she held back to watch the king stand. One of his personal guards approached to help. The king was clearly unsteady, but he waved the guard away.

King Aegeus stepped off the dais from his throne and limped out through the back door.

Chapter Three

Pen paced as much as she could in the small stone cell. It had a bed and a window, so it wasn't the worst cell she'd been in, but she'd rather be anywhere else. She had let this get too far out of hand, though she was lucky they had glossed over the blood magic charge. King Aegeus probably marked that claim down to the boy's grief and imagination. She might not be lucky next time; anyone accused of magic was sentenced to death almost on the spot. She had to get out.

They had taken her pack and weapons, but she was not defenseless. She approached the door and peered out of the small, barred window. It was dark but she could make out another door like hers directly across the corridor. From this angle she couldn't see any other people.

Pen put her back to the wall beside the door. Digging into her sleeve, into a small hidden pocket, she withdrew a razor. It was too small to be a viable weapon in a fight, but it did the job she needed by slicing open her first finger on her right hand.

She put the razor back and knelt by the door. The side closest to the latch would have been safer, but the wood was tight against the stone. There was a small space between the wood and the floor.

She waited but heard nothing. This could be her only chance of escape, but she risked exposure. She prayed that the corridor was empty.

Willing her blood to move away from the cut, she pulled out a tendril no thicker than a hair. Holding her hand to the bottom of the door, the tendril floated beneath the door. To Pen, moving the blood outside her body felt as natural as moving a limb, but she had to be careful to touch as little as possible. She would get sick if any dirt or toxins got into her system. Not seeing what you were doing didn't help, either. Judging by the placement of the door handle she found on the other side, she could guess where the keyhole was.

She made the tendril rise on the other side of the door and prodded the area under the latch. It took a few tries, each one increasing her chances of being caught, but she finally found the keyhole. The tendril went inside it, and she felt around the gears, as if they were touching her own skin.

Pen felt the grooves and tumblers of the lock mechanism. There were four tumblers in this lock, not too difficult, but it would have been easier is she had been able to see it. It took several tries, but the lock finally clicked, and she withdrew the tendril. She collected the blood into a ball above her hand and used her sleeve to wipe away as much dirt and grease as possible. She then drew it back into her finger. The cut didn't heal immediately, but she stopped the bleeding through willpower.

The door swung outward into the corridor, which was blessedly empty. The pathway to the right opened up but there was a shadow of a figure looming on the wall. Pen closed the door silently and headed left. The route proved fruitless, since it just led down to more cells. She didn't want to risk the chance of getting stuck. She turned and went back; it wasn't a long corridor, and there were only five cells on either side.

The archway to the end opened to a small room for the guards on duty. A lantern cast a shadow on a table littered with food. The man sitting there was flipping through a deck of cards. It didn't look like he was playing any particular game. He hadn't heard her approach, but he was facing in her direction. She hid by the corner of the archway. The exit was directly across from her, mocking her.

Pen drew from the cut on her finger again. The blood lowered to the floor and snuck around the corner. She hoped that the man was paying enough attention to his cards that he wouldn't notice the movement. She stole a peek around the stone. He was reading one card closely. The tendril continued to stretch along the floor, hugging the wall, and it now gathered in the far corner behind him.

Sending more blood to thicken the end, she formed it into a thin arrowhead and hardened the point. She raised the arrowhead behind the man. Having to watch to make sure she angled the arrow correctly left her in the light and exposed.

The man tossed his card onto the table, sighing and scowling. He sat back in the chair, ruining her angle. He spotted her, shouted, and made to rise. Pen stepped out from the archway, swung the arrowhead and stuck him deep in the eye into his skull.

He slumped back in the chair, staring at her, but even his uninjured eye didn't see her any longer.

She approached the dead man, cleaning her blood in her shirt. He had a short sword at his belt, along with keys to all the cells. Unsure how to cover the evidence of her magic, she took the sword but left the keys. Anyone who found him might think he was negligent and forgot to lock her in. The wound in his eye might be a problem; it was too small to have been made by a blade. Pen unsheathed the short sword and stuck it in his eye. The blade cleaved into his cheekbone, and the force drove the body into the wall. Pen wrenched the sword free with a sickening, wet sound, and the body fell to the floor. She kicked the table. Soup sloshed out of the bowl, and the lamp overturned but stayed lit. Now it would appear as though there had been a struggle.

After cleaning the blood from the blade on the dead man's tunic, Pen strapped the sword to her belt. Through the exit was a stairway leading upward to a thick, dark wood door with hinges that stretched across its width. Fortunately, this door wasn't locked. Pen opened it slowly and spotted two guards chatting at the end of the passage. She squared her shoulders and left the safety of the doorway, turning right. The guards paid her no mind. If they saw her, they probably thought she was a servant. She counted on that invisibility. Servants didn't walk around with weapons, but she could claim she was delivering it from the blacksmith to a noble. She'd think of something if need be; she just had to control the nervous hum in her veins.

A series of stone hallways and another staircase took her up to another room, another door. Holding on to her innocent maid idea, Pen opened the door, stepped through, and found herself at the base of a tower attached to the keep. She paused to breathe in the cool, damp air. The sky was gray overhead; it might rain again.

The courtyard wasn't big, but it was a reprieve from the cold stone corridors. Pen stood beneath an overhang held up by limestone columns. Several people moved about, servants and guards mostly, though one side of the courtyard was taken up by the blacksmith's workshop. She could hear the steady clang of metal striking metal, and nearby horses. The stables must be close.

Pen spotted Captain Tellus across the courtyard.

He had his back to her, talking to a couple of men, probably giving orders. She ducked her head and walked quickly in the other direction. She had always found that if one walks with a purpose in mind, or at least if one looks like it, people tend to leave one alone. It would have been true this time, too, had she not turned a corner into an open pathway and ran right into someone. She let out a sharp yell of surprise as she staggered back. A hand shot out and caught her arm before she fell.

Pen looked up, and her nerves sparked into fear. Delmore held her arm.

Before he could let out more than a surprised, "Hey," she punched him in the gut. He doubled over, coughing, and she took off behind him.

Some people were looking her way after seeing Delmore crumple. They spotted her. Tellus was one of them; the noise must have caught his attention. Pen heard him shouting, "Stop her!"

She had a slight head start, and most of the people were startled. That did not last long. One man made a grab for her, but she ducked in time, weaving around another guard, but barreled into a group of servants and a stable boy in the process. A girl carrying a basket of linens fell, nearly taking Pen with her, but Pen kept her footing and pressed on.

She headed to the nearby barracks. A group of trainees came out of the two story stone building to investigate the commotion. Pen veered left, hopped onto a barrel on a supply cart, vaulted up to a window on the second storey of the building, then clambered onto the roof. It was made of red clay tiles that slipped and cut her hands, but she made it up. Pausing only for a second to breathe, Pen saw at least two dozen men below. Some circled the building under Tellus's orders, and a couple of others were stringing bows. One aimed a crossbow at her.

"Don't kill her, damn it!" Tellus wrenched the crossbow up as the man pulled the trigger. The bolt flew towards her. The slight rush of air, along with the movement in her hair over the shoulder, was the only indication the man had missed her neck with that bolt.

She turned and ran along the tiles. Arrows clattered on the tiles around her feet, but none struck home. They must have been aiming at her legs on Tellus's orders. She jumped a narrow alley, landing on the neighboring building; this roof was blessedly flat. Her heart pounded against her ribcage like a wild animal, and her veins sung with anticipation, but she refused to draw any weapons or shields with so much attention on her.

The building ended at a road beneath her. The city was built on a hill, so the road was too far down for her to survive the landing. There was a window directly below her, though. She gripped the edge of the roof, jumped, and swung. Her feet just barely touched the sill. Kicking in the glass, she scrambled into the building.

She found herself inside a low ceilinged attic. There were crates and barrels everywhere that reeked of dyes; it was probably a tannery. There might have been a place to hide, but given how close the guards were and the noise she made breaking the window, she still wasn't safe. She had to get away from the central keep and barracks.

She opened the only door, then stopped. There was a child in the room beyond, a little boy maybe four years old, playing with blocks and toy soldiers on the floor. He watched her with wide blue eyes. Pen froze, her own son had eyes just as big but they were dark like his fathers. He would have been around this boy's age.

She left the boy where he was and ran to the next door, which led to a landing and stairs leading downward. She could hear voices approaching, no doubt coming to investigate the noise. She flew down the stairs three at a time, rounded a corner, and knocked over a woman wearing brown leather gloves stained blue at the tips.

Pen rushed to another window at the end of the hallway and, this time, used the latch to open it properly. The shouting of the guards was getting closer. Twenty feet below the window was a short wall that separated this tier of the city from the one below, then another fifty feet down to a cobblestone road. The sky had opened and a mist like rain fell.

Pen hoisted herself through the window, stretching herself as long as possible to gain length to the wall, and dropped. The wall only allowed for a foot wide stretch of stone. Bracing her feet wide and leaning onto the outside of the building, she paused to thank the gods that she hadn't toppled over.

Her reprieve was short lived.

Arrows struck the wall to her left. Daring a look, Pen saw six guards and Tellus on the road below.

"You stay there, and I might be lenient," Tellus shouted.

Pen shuffled right as quickly as the foot wide ledge would allow. She was exposed on the wall, but she knew how to keep her balance. She ran along the ledge, the guards close behind, with Tellus barking orders to cut her off.

The wall descended and curved to the next tier. It looped back on itself, which would leave her facing the guards. Pen crouched and slid partway in the slickness the rain had left on the stones. She vaulted off the wall at the last moment and sailed through the air. She realized that part of the shouting she could hear was her own screams. The road ended and she continued to fall into the tree line that stretched down the hill, dropping away from her.

Leaves and branches filled her vision and raked every inch of her skin as she fell. The skeletal branches left cuts as though from bird talons. One last branch broke under her weight as she hit it full force. That branch had slowed her down enough for her to tuck and roll. The landing was harder, as rocks and dirt ground into the wounds. She rolled to avoid breaking any bones, then landed on her stomach.

Her ears rang, and every sound seemed to come through cotton. Was she drowning, had she landed in a pool of water? She tried to open her eyes, but everything swam. She was still breathing, so she hadn't landed in water. She gulped a couple of mouthfuls of air, then forced herself to her knees. Her vision cleared enough, and her hearing was coming back, but too slowly for her liking. She forced herself to her feet and continued forward. It was that or die.

The grove in which she had landed was wild with birds and small game. They were probably kept here as a reprieve from city life, though the dark stone castle with its red banners still loomed overhead. Pen's whole body ached and bled from dozens of cuts. She was glad nothing was broken, but her left ankle throbbed with every step.

The grove ended, and she found herself in a graveyard. The rain was falling more heavily now, painting the tombstones with dark tears. She had to get out of the rain and find shelter. She couldn't continue on like this, not after that fall.

An archway in the side of the hill led to darkness. Its gate stood wide open, beckoning her to safety. Pen smiled at the irony of hiding with the dead when she might join them soon. She entered the crypt and pulled the gate shut behind her. Her hearing had returned, but the bones in here were quiet. She had slipped from Tellus's grasp for the moment.

Pen turned away from the rain streaked light and stumbled farther into the crypt. The passage branched in several directions, with walls filled with niches and alcoves. Each space held an urn or a coffin. The stench of the fresh residents did not bother her much; this was not the first crypt she'd slept in. She hoped it wouldn't be the last.

She turned left, then right at the first opportunity, in order to simplify the directions back to the entrance. She entered a small room with a single wooden coffin in its center. This individual must have had wealth to afford his or her own room. She noticed that the lid was not secured. Rusty, broken nails lay on the floor around the coffin.

Pen knelt and opened the lid. A skeleton lay inside, clothed in a purple robe. Wealthy indeed, though any jewels he may have been buried with were gone. The grave robbers had better use for them then the dead did.

Nausea bit at the back of Pen's throat, but she couldn't risk being found. She crawled in beside the skeleton and closed the lid.

Chapter Four

Pen hoped it was only the delusions of a fever setting in, but she could feel the dead watching her. She was cold all over, and every scratch and break in her skin screamed at her. She could feel her blood trying to leak out, but she willed it back. She would not die of blood loss as long as she was conscious. She could not work her magic while asleep, though her blood sometimes seemed to have a mind of its own. The strangest moment was when it first manifested. She had been born with this gift, though it had acted like a curse ever since it awakened within her, three months ago. The cold sank to her bones as she shivered, pushing away the memory. She couldn't relive it, not now, although it played anyway at the black edges of her consciousness.

Pen didn't know how much of the darkness was from the crypt or if her vision was fading. She had knocked her head when she had landed earlier. She lay on her side, facing away from her companion so she could only see the lines in the wood of the coffin wall, but even they were beginning to blur. The grooves in the wood seemed to swirl, merge, then separate and continue on.

She could feel her consciousness slipping as the blood started to seep from her wounds, soaking her tunic. A drop of crimson filled her eye, it must be from a gash on her head. She moved to wipe it way, but her arm screamed in pain. She gritted her teeth to prevent the scream from escaping.

Her mind grew dark after that. Everything grew soft and black, even the ribcage of the skeleton poking at her back. She lost consciousness and dreamed of that moment with her family, her child.

A sudden stumbling noise and a man cursing woke Pen from her uneasy rest. Fever hadn't set in yet, but she was dizzy from the blood loss. She couldn't draw the blood back now, because she hadn't been the one to draw it out. Another voice joined the man who cursed. She couldn't make out the words, because they were too far away. She could only lie there with her dead friend and wait. The voices grew louder as they came closer. Her head was fuzzy, but she could make out their words.

"This is insane, who in their right minds would hide in here?" one man asked.

"Honestly, I would if I were on the run," another voice answered. "Besides, the captain said to check everywhere."

The other man cursed again.

"You know he'd have our hides if we didn't look."

"I know, I know." He was clearly irritated. Pen would have laughed if her heart wasn't in her throat.

"Open every coffin that can be opened," the second man ordered.

"Are you serious?"

"Yes!"

"The goddess Nyx will have our souls for this," the first replied.

Pen could hear them moving among the bones and the creak of old coffins as they searched. She was too dizzy to shake, but that actually helped. She could force herself to be alert, but she couldn't draw any more blood; it would make her more lightheaded. Hardly daring to move, she reached to her side for the short sword.

It was gone. Damn belt must have broken off in her fall through the trees, and she hadn't noticed. She reached behind her and grabbed a rib that had broken off her dead companion.

The two men had grown quiet in their search, but the shuffling and grunts told her they were close, maybe only a few feet away. The footsteps fell closer to her coffin. Pen was sure they must be able to hear her heart pounding. The last footfall landed beside her head, and the man was standing right over her.

A sliver of light spilled into the coffin. Pen squinted but didn't move; there were only fingers gripping the lid as the man hesitated. It was most likely the more fearful man, judging by the sounds the other had made down the corridor. She silently screamed at this one to leave.

He took a breath, probably to steady his nerves. He threw open the lid and Pen pounced, digging the rib bone into his neck. She managed to get her hand over his mouth, but not before he released a scream. He stared at her as warm blood sprang around her fingers. He tried to breathe but only choked. Pen left the rib stuck in his flesh and ran out of the crypt.

She headed for the entrance but didn't get more than a few feet before there was a blinding flash of pain on the back of her head, then darkness.

Pen was falling; it was oddly pleasant until she hit the stone floor. Pain flared up the arm she had injured in her fall, which woke the other wounds. Rolling, she saw Captain Tellus slamming the door, leaving her in a smaller dark cell with no windows. The only light came from the crack where the door ended and the floor began.

"Are you mad, Tellus?" Pen recognized Connin's voice from the trial.

"If you don't shut up, I'll lock you in one of these myself," Tellus growled.

"You can't let her gain her strength, she'll just escape again."

"I won't let that happen. Besides, we can't execute her without the king's order. People haven't been dying from the hangings anyway!"

"Use a longer rope or the blade, then. And we don't need the king's bloody order on this; you've sentenced more petty criminals and thieves to the noose than he bothers with. It's your job to thin the herd for him, right?" Contempt dripped from Connin's voice.

What did Tellus mean, people hadn't been dying at the hangings?

"Not with an accusation this big. The guard on duty lost his eye because she stabbed him with her blood." Pen's heart jumped to her throat, the guard was alive! "And that boy said she made her blood move when she killed his family. She could be the next Blood Warrior."

Connin's laugh did not quell the chill that raced up Pen's back. She cursed herself for being so careless about the guard and the travelers. But how could the guard be alive? The blade went at least three inches deep into his brain; she felt it crush his skull.

"There hasn't been a Warrior in decades," Connin scoffed.

"That doesn't mean there will never be another."

"So on a hunch you're going to bother the king, who's dying, about a couple of petty attacks."

"There were witnesses!"

"An imaginative boy and a guard probably drunk at his post again."

"So you say we just kill her."

"She obviously lied at the trial. Her attempted escape proves her guilt, and she nearly killed two men. One will probably be dead by the end of the day, with that bone in his neck. Why defend her now?"

"I'm defending the king's justice. We don't execute until the crime is clear."

"Attempted murder isn't clear enough? It was before. What's changed, Tellus?"

"The witnesses—"

"Are in shock and don't know what they saw."

Silence. Pen didn't have to see Tellus to know he was seething. She managed to sit up against the wall. She listened with increasing anxiety as they argued over her fate.

"She stays here until the king is told." Tellus's voice allowed no further argument.

"We should use the blade. Quicker than the noose, and there's no room for error."

Pen was surprised Tellus didn't punch Connin; she just heard footsteps receding down the corridor.

Chapter Five

The day was overcast again. Pen hoped it would be a downpour and drown them all. Every step rattled with the chains they bound her in. Two guards in red Stymphalian colors escorted her from her cell to the gray courtyard. Her only satisfaction was that two guards were used to watch one woman. They were afraid of her.

Not that she could do much at this point. They had drugged her enough that she could hardly speak. She couldn't fight anyway, because her wounds had healed over, and she had no way of cutting herself. Her razor was in her cuff, but the chains were blocking the pocket. Her brain was filled with cotton, but she kept her head up, staring down anyone who met her eye.

These people were here for entertainment. The courtyard was filled with spectators for the day's executions. Many of them even had brought food. These people were going to watch the last Blood Warrior die, and they didn't even know it.

Pen let herself think of her family. She only had a few strides left in Ichorisis, so she allowed herself a moment of good memories. Soon she'd be in Skiachora, and no one knew what the dead did there once Nyx took their souls.

Pen walked through the crowd and saw the executioner's platform loom over the heads of the onlookers. The strongest image in her mind was of Alard playing with the blocks Arch had carved. She would see them again sooner than she thought. She would see her father again too; that actually made her glad under the circumstances. Pen might even meet her mother, who had died in childbirth, so Pen's father had to raise her alone as they traveled.

Her father hadn't been the previous Blood Warrior; he would have told her. Everyone knew that the next Warrior in the bloodline gained his or her powers when the previous one died. Pen would have come into her powers when her father died two years ago. Her mother must have been the Warrior before her, then, but kept it hidden. Given the persecution of the entire bloodline over a hundred years ago, it made sense that she would have hidden her powers. Pen's father had described her mother as just a rancher's daughter with high spirits. Pen wondered if he knew about her magic.

Alard was to be the next Blood Warrior after her death. Now the entire line was dead, and Pen couldn't help but blame herself. Her son was dead because of her.

She reached the steps up to the platform. A tall guillotine stood waiting for her, the executioner standing beside it. Her bravery faltered when she saw the blade. It was a foot long at its shortest end and angled to create a vicious point.

She hadn't realized she had stopped until the guard on her left nudged her forward. It almost knocked her over, but she caught herself. She may have wanted to see her family, but basic survival instinct was holding her back. That, and the fact that she would be letting the Blood Warrior, the legend, die.

The guards gripped her arms and began pulling her up the steps.

"No!"

Pen struggled and almost slipped from their grasp, but the chains around her feet got in the way. They dragged her up the platform toward the guillotine. She tried to break their grip, not caring that there was no point to running through a crowd, laden with chains. More people were watching now, watching her squirm in fear. She hated all of them for enjoying this.

The guards ordered her to lie down on the table, but she fought them. She tried cutting her hand on the chain, even lunging for a guard's short sword. If she could get one pinprick, she could easily dispatch all of them and run.

Pain erupted over her left temple, and everything went black. She sagged, dazed, convinced they had just killed her right then, but the throbbing pain convinced her otherwise. She opened her eyes to double vision and felt for blood on her head, but there was none.

It took two guards and the executioner to pin her down on the table and tie her in place. The executioner didn't wear a hood, just a simple hide and leather apron. He looked bored. Pen wanted to gouge his eyes out for it. He secured the block of wood, keeping her head still.

Pen lay on her back. She should have been on her stomach, but she refused to complain. It would only cause the audience more joy to see her beg. It was her own fault, anyway, for not fighting hard enough. The polished blade hung above her. She wanted to close her eyes but couldn't.

From the corner of her eye Pen saw the executioner take hold of the rope holding the blade. She had to close her eyes; she didn't want to see it fall. Her heart beat like an enraged hummingbird.

The executioner let the rope go, and Pen saw light flash on the steel as it raced to greet her.

Breathing hurt. It felt like tiny razor blades were inside her throat. The only thing Pen was conscious of was that pain, and the fact that she couldn't see. She lay on her side. She didn't know where she was or if others were close by. Everything was silent and unnerving. This wasn't right. There was no way of knowing how long she'd been here.

After some time (An hour? A day? She had no idea) Pen heard noises. The rusty hinges of a door, footsteps coming closer, and then they stopped. There was a pause, then the sound of wood touching a hard surface and soft shuffling.

A hand touched her shoulder and rolled her onto her back. She realized then that her hands were bound. She couldn't have moved them anyway; it felt like her bones were replaced with lead. She wanted to get away, to run. Her heart beat faster, but that was all that moved.

A spoon touched her lips, and tasteless soup slid down her throat. Whoever was feeding her was careful to give her only small amounts so she didn't choke, but it caused more agony in her throat. The razors were burning white hot now, but she couldn't scream.

After a dozen spoonfuls of soup, the razors of pain left her breathless. She vowed to kill whoever had left her in this blind, limp, agonizing state.

Her vision returned slowly, but she was still weak and bound. Having no way to measure time, she had no idea if she'd been there for days or weeks. Her caretaker had returned four more times to feed her when she was blind, so she guessed it had been maybe four days. There were no windows, only a thick door. When she finally saw the flickering light from under the door, though the rest of the room was dark, she knew her vision had returned.

The caretaker came and went three more times. Each time she tried to speak, but she could only croak. Whatever they put in her food prevented her from speaking too.

The scene at the executioner's block kept playing in her head. She could only remember the angled blade above her, and watching as it raced to greet her. There had been only blackness after that. No pain, no sound, no memory, only darkness. She had thought she would at least see Nyx, the goddess who was said to take your soul as you died, but even the gods had forsaken her. Something must have halted the execution. She must have fainted, and for some reason they hadn't proceeded with the execution. It would be cruel and petty not to continue just because she fainted. Someone must have caught the blade in time.

She felt almost as bad as she had during the first few days of experimenting with her blood magic. After burying Arch and Alard she had left their home. Life was always safer that way, and given her nomadic traveling with her father, it was all she had known before she had become a housewife. Living meal to meal, not having to worry about anyone, and not having anyone close enough to hurt you.

Lying there sick and weak reminded her of those first times she practiced. She hadn't wanted to at first but she had known she couldn't run from herself. The power was simple enough. She had found she could form any shape she needed, and that she could sharpen any edge or point.

Her first attempt at forming a knife had been easy. The blood was an extension of herself and reacted instantly with her thoughts. Keeping her connection with the knife, she had grown it into a short sword, then again into a two-handed broadsword. She had forgotten her grief for a moment when she realized that the weight of the weapon hadn't much changed. The broadsword was awkward but she had been able to hold it with one hand. She had forced it to grow more, wanting to see how big it could get.

She hadn't seen how big it had become. The next thing she had known was waking up on the forest floor. She had felt weak and nauseous. There had been a long puddle of blood beside her, where the sword had been. She had lost control when she fainted and it had melted.

Pen had known then that the blood wasn't being created by itself, it was being drawn from her own body. Afterwards, she was always mindful of how much she used at one time to avoid blood loss.

Given her previous escape attempts, she could understand why they had left her here, drugged, alone and bound. But why keep her alive in the first place?

After what might have been a week, or a month for all she knew, two men opened the cell door. The light from the single torch blinded her as they cut the bonds from her legs and lifted her to her feet. They left the shackles on her hands. By then her eyes had adjusted, and she saw Connin in the doorway.

"Come," he said to the guards, barely glancing at her. He turned and disappeared from the archway. One of her escorts nudged her on the back. It took all of Pen's willpower to stay upright, even if his touch was light. The guards watched her warily with weapons drawn. Pen staggered forward and followed Connin.

After a few minutes, when they had arrived at a different part of the castle. Instead of wood and rugged stones lining the corridors carved stone was used and decorated with tapestries and rich paintings. Connin stopped before a set of dark oak doors. He opened one slowly and ushered Pen inside. She wondered if he was leading her to some other means of imprisonment or death, when she came up short in the new room.

She was in a parlor furnished with a table, desks, tapestries, ornaments of war, and a fireplace big enough for a tall man to stand in. The fire was roaring, heating the room, and the king was sitting in a high backed chair before it.

Connin gripped Pen's arm hard, making her hiss through her teeth. He pulled her forward, tossing her to the king's feet. Pen fell to her knees but kept her composure, for what it was worth. She was weak, but the walk had invigorated her a bit, and she refused to show Connin or the king fear. They would pounce on it like hounds upon a fox.

"Pick her up, Connin," King Aegeus ordered. His voice was firm but it cracked at the end.

"Your Grace?" Connin said. Pen enjoyed hearing him confused.

"Set her on the chair." Aegeus gestured to the one beside him. "And release her hands, damn it."

Connin hesitated.

"Now!" the king barked. Pen was impressed that his order hadn't ended in a bloody cough.

Connin lifted her by the shoulders and practically threw her in the seat. He then withdrew a keyring and unshackled her bonds.

"Now leave us," Aegeus said.

"I'm sorry, but I must protest, my liege, she is a convicted criminal, a monster," Connin argued.

"If you don't, I'll have you thrown into a cell with her."

Connin swallowed his pride and left.

Pen and Aegeus sat facing the fire together. She waited for him to speak first, but he only watched the fire. Curiosity got the better of her caution.

"I *could* kill you," she said. "Why have us left alone?"

"I wish you could. I can feel my insides rotting."

Pen believed him. Aegeus sat slumped in the chair with a blanket over his legs, despite the heat from the fire. He looked like a ragged skeleton under his regal clothes.

"You know why I had to keep you drugged?" he asked.

"I would have escaped otherwise," Pen answered smoothly.

"Aye, and everyone is terrified after your stunt at the execution. Must have been impressive, to be honest, though you understand why I couldn't attend." Pen noticed the bitterness in his voice.

She wanted to reply in kind but decided it was a bad idea. "Impressive from where you stood, maybe, not on the chopping block with a blade above your neck."

"It wasn't just above your neck. Your head rolled."

Her reply died on her tongue. How could her head have been lopped off if she sat here now? Was she dead and this was a cruel afterlife? Her heart still beat, she knew. She was alive, but what he said didn't make sense.

Aegeus watched as she floundered for words. He sat up a little straighter. "What do you remember?"

Pen cleared her throat; it still felt like she had swallowed glass. "I remember being dragged to the guillotine. I saw the blade… fall. Then I woke up in the black cell."

"What do you feel now?"

"What do you mean?" Her heart was alive alright; it was beating against her ribs.

"When you woke up. What did you feel?"

Pen hesitated. "As if there was a rope of fire around my neck, and as if I'd swallowed glass."

Aegeus sat back and watched her, stunned yet fascinated.

"My head was severed from my body?" Pen forced herself to put the idea into words. It helped her grasp the idea better.

"Yes." It was eerie how calm the king seemed.

Pen shuddered, despite the fire. "How? How did I come back?"

Aegeus described the reports from the execution. That the blade of the guillotine exploded. Shards of metal and chunks of wood bombarded the crowd as they screamed.

One shard of metal stuck in the executioner's arm when he shielded his face.

People watched as tendrils of crimson strings grew from her neck where her head would have been. There were hundreds of snake like strings swinging around. Most of them struck the guards nearby, and the executioner, aiming for their necks. All of them fell choking on their own blood. Some of the tendrils attacked the first people in the crowd in the same manner, causing the rest to scream and panic. Anyone who approached the madness was attacked by the sentient strings. The tendrils seemed to calm after a time and picked up the head. The king described it as an image of a squid and its tentacles he had seen once in a book. They were almost tender when picking up her severed head and sticking themselves into the base of it. The tendrils withdrew back into her body, drawing the head back onto the neck with a small squish. Then she choked back a breath.

As he spoke, unease rose in Pen's heart, along with the fear. She did her best to not let it show, but she hadn't noticed her hand creep up to touch her neck. There she felt a scab ringing her skin. Dread took hold as well; there was no denying her identity now, if her blood had attacked the crowd.

"One more strange thing is that despite the wounds you inflicted, even through the heart, no one died in that attack."

"No one died?"

"Not one."

Relief allowed her to breathe. How was she not dead, or the people at the execution? What happened to the man she stabbed in the crypt with the bone? Or the guard in the first cell? He'd only lost an eye. Pen was sure the sword had pierced his brain. Or that family of bandits for that matter, what happened to them? She might not possess all of the puzzle pieces, but there were enough.

"Why aren't people dying?"

"I have no idea, but most people have been seeing it as a gift from the gods. I don't." Aegeus's voice was hard.

Pen touched her neck again, remembering the pain. "So why call me here?"

"Because I need to get you out of the city but still keep you in check—" He coughed. He caught the blood in the handkerchief, but it was a shocking amount. He grunted, then took a moment to collect himself from the obvious pain. Pen could understand why he didn't see this change as a blessing.

"Why get me out of the city?" Pen asked, not following his logic. "Keeping me locked up would be safer." Not that she wanted that fate.

"I'm sending you to the Acheron. You're to follow the river upstream to find its source in Skiachora. You'll most likely find Maniodes's castle too, you could ask him or help."

Pen scoffed. "No one has ever found the source, or the fabled land of the gods."

"You will, and you will go into the source, find out why none of us are dying, and fix it."

She was stunned. "You want me to talk to the gods?"

"Don't talk to me like I'm senile. I'm dying, not crazy."

"Technically, you're not dying."

Aegeus half laughed, half coughed, and gave a small smile. "Maybe I *am* crazy."

Pen felt for the dying man. His life couldn't have been easy, and now his death wouldn't be either.

"You think the rumors are true, then? That the source of the river leads to the gods?"

"Rivers have to start somewhere, and so do stories. I've never put much stock in the gods myself, but I would not have believed a woman could survive a beheading."

Pen didn't have a response for that. She didn't believe in the gods either, only men and their actions. She touched her neck again. "Why send me?"

"Because you're the Blood Warrior. They say you're half divine yourself: a demigod. You're born of Maniodes, the son of Nyx. If anyone could reach them, it would be a Warrior."

"What if I refuse? I may be the Blood Warrior, but I'm no demigod. Those are only stories."

"I could lock you back up again and let this problem continue to fester."

"I'll break out."

"That worked well last time."

"I don't have to restrict my powers now."

"So people will see you as a villain and hunt you down. Bounties are easy to make."

"They're also easy to avoid."

"But with everyone hunting you, there will be no safe haven. Remember, I control this city and have high connections in the others."

"I don't care about that." She was already the worst kind of person, why not have all of Ichorisis hate her too?

Aegeus was quiet for a while, watching her. "I believe you."

Pen couldn't respond. She was tempted to jump out of the window into the night. Whether to her freedom or death, she didn't know. It would have to be her escape, if she couldn't die.

"If we are to trust one myth, why not another?" He coughed again. "That the gods will grant us a favor if we help them."

"Who says we're helping them? If this is divinely brought, who are we to interfere?"

"Who says we wouldn't be?" he countered. "Humans' greatest danger is curiosity in some ways, but it can't be helped, curiosity is part of our nature."

"So would the favor then go to you for sending me? Are you going to ask them to finally let you die?" It was cold, but Pen didn't care.

"If you are successful, I wouldn't have to," he said. "Besides, you know who you'll have to find, given the situation."

Nyx, the goddess of death. The myths said she took the souls of those dying so they could finally be free to enter Skiachora. Since no one was dying, it would make sense to start with her. And she was the mother of the other gods; at the very least she would have a lead.

King Aegeus continued, "I'm sure she would be happy to grant you favor, if you help her in some way. Maybe she can bring back a loved one, like in the stories."

His voice was cold and sarcastic, but the words punched Pen in the heart. She had heard those stories too, that Nyx could bring back the dead.

She pushed down the budding hope. "The dead can't come back."

"Not by human means, but Nyx is the goddess of death herself. She could pull a few strings."

Pen tried to stamp out the sense of hope, but it had taken root. She could save her son and husband.

"Why send me, though? You said you had to keep me in check, for the city's sake. It can't just be because I can move my blood."

"You're not going alone. I'm sending my captain of the guard with you. To make sure you don't run off on me."

"Captain Tellus?"

"Yes," he said matter-of-factly. "He's my best soldier."

Pen couldn't do this, following a myth in the hope that there was even a grain of truth. The dead were dead, and they couldn't come back. But the alternative was prison again.

"Who did you lose?" Clearly Aegeus had been able to follow some of her thoughts.

Pen almost didn't answer. "My son and husband."

"How old was your boy?"

"Three," she managed to choke out.

"You might get him back."

Pen stared at the fire, willing the tears away, trying and failing not to think about the time he burned his little hand trying to help her clean their fireplace. He hadn't realized the iron poker was hot and grabbed the wrong end.

What if it was true? What if the source of the Acheron led to Skiachora and the gods? If Pen could find Nyx, she could find out why people couldn't die. She didn't care about being a hero, but this *was* monumental. She might even find Maniodes, the ruler of Skiachora. His castle was said to be down there with the dead. At the very least she'd get out of that cell. She could escape from Tellus somehow and be free. She didn't care about a bounty.

"I'll do it," she said, with steel in her voice. She didn't want to admit it was for her family; the failure would crush her, but hope bloomed nonetheless.

"Good, because you leave at first light."

Chapter Six

Tellus paced around his apartments in the barracks, packing his saddlebags. It was the middle of the night, but he'd just received word from King Aegeus himself that he was to accompany the woman to the Acheron. He dug his hand into his dark green hair, wondering if his friend had lost his mind. It made sense, but it wasn't easy to swallow. He had been watching the king decay slowly, and he could do nothing. Tellus remembered when it had started as a slight cough that deepened, yet Aegeus had insisted he was fine. Now Tellus watched as his friend was racked with pain and blood loss every day. That amount of pain was enough to drive anyone mad.

An expedition to the source of the Acheron was something else entirely. Tellus wouldn't have believed the king's theory about people's inability to die, but he'd seen the ring around the woman's neck, though he wasn't at the execution. There were the other executions to consider as well. He had seen people to be hanged until dead, but the bodies would struggle. He would listen to them choke as they were being strangled. None of them gasp their final breath. After ten minutes for the first man twitching on the rope Tellus cut him down and had him imprisoned again. They tried to continue with the days executions but all had the same result. There had been other stories as well; the man who had been stabbed with the rib was healing. He knew the implications of this mission.

He'd refused at first, forgetting his place, but he was one of the few who could. Aegeus had insisted Tellus always be honest with him after his father had passed and he'd become king. If Tellus completed this mission, his friend would die. Aegeus was blunt and said that was the point. Tellus insisted he at least wait for his heir to be born, to buy him time. Aegeus said the journey alone would take a few months, and his son would be born by then.

Tellus would have given anything to save his friend, but hope eventually gave out. His friend was dying, and there was nothing he could do but make his passing easier, or at least possible. So he agreed, vowing to protect Queen Aethra and their child.

He remembered when he had first met Aegeus. He had been only eight years of age and helping in the kitchens. His mother had been a scullery maid working there to earn room and board for her son and herself. Tellus helped when he was needed, usually peeling potatoes or cleaning pots, but most of the time he explored the outskirts of the castle and the city.

The guards never let him inside the castle. He once tried sneaking in during a festival to see the royal family. The guards caught him, dragged him out, beat him, and left him in the alley. It took Tellus almost two hours to get back to the kitchens, slowed by the bruises and too afraid to run into any other guards.

It was night when he finally found his mother. He told her what happened as she dressed his wounds.

"You shouldn't have tried in the first place," she said. She wasn't angry but stern, even a little sad. Her green hair was tied back in a bun, and he saw how tired she was.

"I just wanted to see the king and queen," little Tellus said, wincing at the bruise under his eye.

"I know." She held his arm. "But those people don't want us around. They don't want us in sight, anyway."

"Why, because they're cleaner?"

His mother laughed. Seeing her happy made him feel leagues better. He knew he had troubled her and didn't want her to be sad.

"In a way," she said, gently hugging him. "Promise me you won't try that again. We are lucky to be where we are."

He promised that he would never bother the guards or try for the castle again, and he never did. She died five months later after she had a cough that worsened to the point that she could barely breathe without wheezing.

The cook let him stay as long as he kept working to earn his keep. He did everything the cook needed, always afraid of ending up on the streets. He had nowhere else to go and no family to take him in. His father ran off before he was born, and his mother never spoke of him. He probably didn't know Tellus existed.

He left well enough alone; while living in the kitchens, he kept his promise to his mother and stayed out of trouble as best he could.

One day Tellus was peeling potatoes and carrots outside because it was too hot to stay inside with the ovens. He never liked potatoes because they always left his hands slimy. Three boys came up to him asking what he was doing.

"Peeling potatoes," he replied.

Tellus kept his eyes down as his mother and the cook taught him. These boys were older than him by a few years and richly dressed. He didn't want trouble, but he sensed it coming, from their clothes and their sneers.

"You're supposed to kneel to those better than you, boy," said the tallest one, who had orange and yellow hair.

The others behind their leader snickered.

Tellus knew about most of the noble families through gossip, but he didn't know this boy. Even at eight he could tell this boy was no more than a bully, but he was a foot taller than Tellus.

He got off his stool and knelt, thinking of his mother, though his blood boiled.

"Good," the orange haired lad said. He picked up the bucket of potato and carrot skins and dumped them over Tellus's head, covering his hair and shoulders.

"Now, clean up the mess you made." The other boys laughed louder.

Tellus gritted his teeth and glared at the bully. The bully faltered for a second, and Tellus wished he took that chance. But he picked up the bucket and started putting the skins back.

A boot plunged into his stomach. The world went red and airless as Tellus coughed around the pain. The bully kicked the bucket away.

"I said pick up the skins!" he yelled.

Tellus barely heard while he tried to force air back into his lungs. He glared at the bully, realizing the peeling knife was still in his hand.

"Hey!"

Tellus was about to stand, and the bully was about to kick him again, when another boy ran between them and pushed the bully back. The new kid was smaller than the bully, but he had enough force to make the bully step back. Tellus might not have known the bully, but he recognized the prince by his coarse black hair and the family crest at his shoulder. The bully knew him too.

The bully looked like he was about to wet himself, even though Aegeus was younger than him. His friends clearly wanted to run too. Harming or even insulting the king's son would be an act of treason, punishable by death.

"Why were you attacking him?" Prince Aegeus demanded. Thinking back now, Tellus saw that it was obvious even then how forceful he would be as king.

"He attacked us, Your Grace," the bully said. One of his friends nodded while the other couldn't move. "He threatened us with that dagger."

The peeling knife was no more than an inch long, but Tellus dropped it like it was a scorpion. It was his word against theirs, the poor kitchen boy against three noble children. He was as good as dead.

The prince actually laughed. "You're lying. I watched the whole thing behind that pillar. You made him kneel, then you kicked him."

The bully faltered. Tellus could breathe again. He couldn't comprehend that the prince was protecting him.

"So what do we do to our betters?" Prince Aegeus asked.

"Uh…" The bully blinked stupidly as he remembered. He knelt before the prince, with the others quickly following.

"Good," Aegeus said. "Now leave."

The orange haired bully and his friends ran.

Tellus burst out laughing at the absurdity. The prince turned to him and smiled. Tellus remembered himself and swallowed the laughter. He knelt before the prince, about to thank him.

"Oh, don't bother with that," Aegeus scoffed. "Get up."

Cautiously, Tellus asked, "What are you doing here?"

His chest seized again at the realization that he had just questioned royalty.

Aegeus shrugged. "I was hungry I was hoping to get a slice of the blueberry pie I saw. Do you want some?"

Tellus blinked. The prince was asking him a sincere question. "Yes, but I'm not allowed until I'm done peeling."

"I'll help you then."

"Why?"

Aegeus retrieved the bucket. "Because then you'll be done faster and we can have pie."

Once everything was peeled and washed, the cook let Tellus and Aegeus each have a huge slice of the pie. Every day afterwards, Aegeus would visit, and they became friends practically overnight. With Aegeus, Tellus was even able to explore the castle on quiet days.

Now, in the keep, Tellus tied his bag together. He'd kept it small to pack light. There were still a couple of hours before dawn, so he lay in bed, hoping to sleep. He dozed restlessly.

Dawn came all too soon. It had felt like only a few minutes had passed when the sun rose and Tellus headed down to the stables, eating a piece of bread and cheese as he walked. He stifled a yawn. The woman, Pen, approached in chains, with Connin and another guard in tow. Pen kept her eyes on the ground, but she didn't look afraid. In fact, there was a small, calm smile. She displayed no sense of nervousness or discomfort of any kind.

As they got closer, Pen looked up at him. The smile stayed but her eyes looked dead. A chill shot up Tellus's neck. He blamed it on the crisp morning. He didn't know which unnerved him more, the dead eyes or the scab ringing her neck, proof that she had defied death itself.

Tellus steeled himself; he was on a mission from his king, and he was not going to let this woman frighten him.

When they came to meet him in the stables just outside the keep, Connin moved to undo Pen's shackles.

"No," Tellus ordered. "Not yet." He held out a hand for the keys.

Connin paused for a moment, then handed them over.

"It'll be a little difficult to get on the horse without my hands," Pen said.

"You'll manage. Now hold them out."

The chain rattled as Pen did as he ordered.

Tellus drew a pair of gloves from a bag attached to his horse. He put them on Pen's hands, noting that they were too large. She'd have to live with it.

"Get on." He gestured to the other horse.

She complied without argument. It was awkward, but she managed to get on by herself.

Tellus was about to mount his own horse when Connin chimed in. "I'm not sure about this."

"Are you questioning the king's orders?" Tellus said.

For once Connin looked away. "No, sir, I'm just surprised by his actions."

Tellus grunted and got in his saddle. "It doesn't matter if you're surprised. The city guard is yours now, *temporarily*. Don't burn the city like last time."

"That wasn't—"

Tellus gathered his reins and Pen's, kicked his horse, and left Connin behind.

Pen didn't say a word as he led her to the south gate.

The guards at the gate recognized Tellus and let him pass uninterrupted. Leaving Stymphalia with its king nearly dead left a poor taste in his mouth, but he started down the south road.

Chapter Seven

"So what did you mean about 'burning the city'?" Pen said. They had been traveling for a short time, and she knew it would be a long journey. Might as well try to talk.

Tellus grimaced at the question. "During a rebellion last year of the mountain tribes, I went to command a section of our army. Connin was left to defend Stymphalia. I wasn't there myself, but the reports stated there was a simple tavern fight that got too rowdy. Connin went to quell it himself and knocked over a lantern. Small mistake, really, but it burned an entire block of houses before it was contained."

"Was anyone hurt?"

"Three dead, one of them a child." His voice was cold.

Pen felt cold too, and wished she hadn't asked. But that did indicate that people were still dying about a year ago.

"So why hide your powers?" Tellus asked.

"Given the persecution of the last few generations of Blood Warriors and their entire extended families, it was safer."

"Fair enough, but that was because you all got power hungry."

"Don't lump me with my ancestors. I didn't even have these powers until a few months ago."

She knew the stories just like everyone else. How the god Maniodes had created Hamia, the first Blood Warrior, and how all of her descendants had the power in their blood. Only one person per generation could be the Warrior, though. Given the family's obvious ties to the gods, they were once worshiped, but that worship turned to skepticism, then to fear, as the years passed. As time went by, people began to question the myths, and their fear became hatred. The reigning Blood Warriors tried to keep the peace, but some saw themselves as superior to everyone else. The people of Ichorisis rebelled and hunted Hamia's descendants. After years of slaughter, everyone believed the bloodline to be dead. Pen's existence was proof that the line still existed.

"Really?" Tellus said intrigued. "I thought they passed on when the previous one died. So there was another in hiding then?"

"No, I think my mother was the last one, but she died giving birth to me. The magic must have lain dormant until I was old enough to handle it."

Maybe her father did know about the hidden Blood Warrior line. Maybe he made sure she knew how to fight so she could incorporate the new blood magic into it.

"That's fascinating."

They continued in silence. The castle of Stymphalia rested on top of the highest hill of three others. The rest of the city-state covered the last two hills and several leagues of plains around them. The hills didn't flatten out completely but did lessen in comparison to the city. Pen and Tellus followed the road winding between hills to the south, heading toward Potamus. There weren't many houses between Stymphalia and Potamus; given how both cities always argued over the land and demanded taxes, no one settled here for long.

There were plenty of travelers going from one city to the next. Tellus had graciously given Pen a blanket to hide her manacles. She had to admit that despite his stern appearance, she could come to like him. He was only following orders, after all; she hoped she wouldn't have to hurt him to escape.

She still wondered if that was even a good idea. There was no hiding her identity now, and she knew it would be easy for King Aegeus to set all of Ichorisis against her.

Then there was the possibility of getting Arch and Alard back. She'd give anything to see Alard smile again, to watch him play in the garden or with the block his father carved for him. Her arms ached to hold her little boy again. She could have Arch back too, she missed the feel of him rolling in his sleep pulling her closer to him unconsciously.

The myths might be skewed, religion and stories easily corrupted, but actions were never wrong. They might be done for the wrong reasons, or not have the required outcome, but they were concrete. Myths might be flawed, but actions spoke of a person's true intent.

As they rode, Tellus pulled bread and dried meat from his saddlebag and handed Pen her share.

Pen took the food in both hands. "Shouldn't we stop to rest the horses?"

"When night falls." He bit off a chunk of meat.

Tellus was definitely a man of action.

Shortly after the sun touched the horizon and began to stain the sky red, Tellus turned their horses off the road. There were no large forests to take cover in, only groupings of maybe a dozen trees, so he picked a shallow area with tall grass and a creek with some birch trees. There was only one more day's ride to Potamus.

He tied his horse to a nearby bush close to the creek and helped Pen off her own.

"Do they have names?" she asked.

Tellus tied her horse beside his own. "Who?"

"The horses," Pen clarified.

"Oh." He paused, taken aback by the question. "I hadn't thought to ask the stable hand."

"We could call them Phobos and Demos," she suggested. She enjoyed throwing him off guard; might as well have some fun on the trip. She also felt closer to animals and wanted to name them.

"Why?" He removed a chain from his pack.

Pen eyed the chain. "We might as well get to know them on the trip. Names make that easier."

"How would naming them let us get to know them?" He looped one end of the chain around a birch tree, locking it back on itself.

"You've never had a pet, have you?"

Tellus stopped working on the chain. "I had a dog once. Xanther."

There was a flicker of something in his eye that was gone before Pen could identify it. He tested the chain's strength, then held the other end. "Come here."

"Really?" She understood why he didn't trust her, but she had no intention of being chained like a dog.

"Yes."

Pen stayed put.

Tellus sighed. "It's going to be a long trip—"

"Which could be a lot more pleasant as long as I'm not tied to a tree," Pen interrupted, "I'll leave the irons on if you want, but if anything were to happen I'd be as good as dead stuck there."

"I'm not going to have you run off on me. Besides, it's five feet long, so there's some leeway."

"Like a leash."

"I wouldn't like it either, but I can't give you the opportunity to escape."

So it was a matter of trust. She had some intention of leaving, of course, but not until this played out more. If there was a chance to get Arch and Alard back, she wanted to take it. Swallowing her pride, she let him shackle her to the tree.

The evening was uneventful, but the stew Tellus cooked over the fire was good. Having to drink it with both hands tied was a pain. Night fell, and he gave her a blanket to curl up beside the fire. This area between the cities was fairly safe, so they both settled down. The extra length of chain at least let her lie down comfortably enough. The air was crisp as she watched the constellation of the cat stalk across the sky.

Snap.

The noise was so small, Pen almost chose to ignore it. Then an odd shadow crossed her peripheral vision. It wasn't an animal; it was too quiet. Pen rolled as if she were still asleep and saw two figures. One was rummaging through the saddlebags while the other kept watch by the road.

Tellus lay beyond the fire, too far for her to wake him. Shouting would scare off the thief, and if she moved too much, the chain would reveal her.

The thief had their coin purse in hand and was rummaging through the next bag. Pen slowly withdrew the razor from her pocket in the sleeve cuff. She had been careful to keep it hidden during her time in the castle dungeon, and the men there never thought to look for a tiny pocket in the sleeve. She cut the back of her wrist where the glove wasn't covering her.

Trying not to touch the dirt, Pen weaved her blood through the grass like a snake toward the thief. Another tendril moved its way toward Tellus at the same time.

Pen trapped the thief first. The blood struck like a snake to the thief's face, covering his mouth with a gag, and made bands around his wrists. He panicked and flailed until Pen grew another tendril, formed a knife, and pressed it to his throat. She could see the whites of his eyes around the dark irises in the firelight. His friend hadn't turned.

She poked Tellus then who woke with a start. Pen pressed blood to his mouth too but removed it after whispering, "Stay quiet."

He took in the scene before him. Pen had sat up to subdue the thief, who was stuck in a contraption of solidified blood. She didn't know if Tellus was furious at her for using her power or that someone had tried to rob them.

Pen was watching the thief when she heard running, then Tellus cursing. He took off after the other figure, who must have seen that his friend was caught and bolted. These people must have been new to robbing people. Some friend.

The bound thief buckled. Distracted by Tellus chasing after the other one, the thin string connecting her to the captive snapped as he pulled back. She hadn't expected him to move with the knife at his neck. He was either braver or more stupid than she had anticipated.

It worked out for him, because with the lost connection, any blood on him melted. It smeared on his face and arms, but he didn't seem to notice as he ran.

Pen sent more blood shooting after him, but he was too quick. She could move the blood as fast as she willed, but he darted around some trees and was gone. She tried to catch him while thickening the tendril into a snake, but draining out that much that fast almost made her pass out. She drew it back and started picking at the lock by her wrists. This mechanism was more challenging than the doors.

Tellus appeared in the firelight, alone, breathing hard from the run.

"Where did the other one go?" he panted.

"He got away behind those trees."

"Damn it!" He ran off in the direction of the trees.

The lock wouldn't give. She pulled at it in frustration, cursing.

Once again, Tellus returned alone. "He had the coins, didn't he?"

"Yes. He got away?"

"Obviously."

She cursed equally at the chains and the thief.

Tellus stood looking at the opened pack, hands on his waist, then at her. "What are you doing?"

As he finished the sentence, the manacles fell from Pen's wrists. She stood there, free, rubbing her chafed skin. Tellus's eyes went from discouraged to battle ready. A hand drifted to the sword at his belt; he'd slept with it on.

"Relax, I'm not going to attack you," Pen said.

"You could have taken those off at any time, couldn't you?"

"Aye."

"Why wait until now?"

"Because we're going to the same place, and I wanted you to trust me in your own time." Pen didn't know if she admired his caution or was irritated by it. This was probably the most he'd spoken to her this entire time.

"So you can run later?" He still didn't believe her. She couldn't really blame him; she'd given him no reason to.

"We are both going to the Acheron for our own reasons," she said, "but if you put those chains on me again, I will break them permanently and go without you. This weird curse means I can't kill you, but I can take your leg."

"Why should I trust your word that you'll come of your own will, if you can so easily threaten me?"

"Because my son and husband are there!" She had no intention of admitting that. Why did she say that? Now her heart was in her throat.

Tellus's expression changed to one of sympathy. She hated it; she didn't deserve it. He gave a slow nod and didn't draw his sword. "So you won't run?"

"No," she managed through a clogged throat.

Tellus nodded again as if reassuring himself. He gathered the open saddlebag and moved it closer to where he'd lain before. He then sat with his back to the fire, watching the road and small woods. Pen sat too, watching his profile.

"I'll stay up and keep watch," he said. "It's almost dawn anyway."

Pen didn't say anything.

After a while she said, "Do you have a handkerchief? Something clean?"

He turned to her, puzzled, then took a small cloth from his vest. He handed it to her.

"What are you going to do?" he asked.

Pen hadn't withdrawn her blood yet. It floated in a ball above her hand, covered in dirt and grease from the lock. Taking off the gloves and using the cloth she wiped the red ball clean, then melted it back into her hand.

"Oh," Tellus said. "Blood poisoning."

"Exactly." She handed back the handkerchief. The cut on her hand wasn't deep; it would be fine without a bandage. She lay down with the woolen blanket. The cat constellation had fallen out of sight, but the twin archers were in the west.

Tellus must have known she wasn't asleep yet, because he asked, "How old was your son?"

Pen took a breath. "Three."

"How did he pass?" His voice was soft.

"It was an accident," she whispered. "I killed him."

Chapter Eight

She had nearly woken up screaming. It wouldn't have been the first time. Tellus hadn't pressed the subject after she admitted to killing her family. He probably judged her as a murderer, and she deserved that. But now there was pity in his eyes when he looked at her, and she hated it. The nightmare just now didn't help either.

The rest of the trek to Potamus was quiet, thankfully. Tellus sat astride Phobos, a solid rusty brown stallion, while Pen had Demos, a pale gray with white on his hindquarters. Pen appreciated that Tellus had accepted the names; she always felt more connected with animals than humans.

The city of Potamus was smaller than Stymphalia but still grand. Having started off as a small fishing village hundreds of years ago, it's only natural defense was the river. It grew quickly due to trade and eventually had enough business and population to warrant bringing down massive blocks of stone from the northern mines, to construct the massive walls that encircled the city, blocking out the plains beyond. The gray blocks were put together with a unique mortar created from the clay of the river, leaving a red grid on the faces of the walls. It looked odd, but that clay provided a flexibility that had survived many siege engines.

Pen and Tellus rode in just as the city gates were closing for the night. While this city was built on the plains, the castle simply known as the Tall Keep was a single tower in the center. It loomed in the distance from the gate and could be seen from the entire city. It was constructed of the same stone as the walls, but these blocks were kept rough on the outside to look more imposing. The city walls, on the other hand, were smooth, so no one could climb them. They were clearly aware of this problem with the tower: on every balcony Pen could see a man dressed in armor marked with the city's blue and brown livery.

The homes were situated along the outside ring of the city, closest to the walls, with shops and markets scattered closer in, mostly by the river. The richer estates and high class inns were even closer to the center of the city, by the Tall Keep.

Tellus led them to an inn called Black Waters by the river, one that had its own stable. It didn't sound pleasant but must get good patronage, judging by the condition it was in.

"How are we going to pay for a room?" Pen asked as they handed their reins to a blond stable boy. All of their money had been stolen the previous night.

"We'll have to sell one of the horses," Tellus replied.

Pen touched Demos once more before he was led away. She had had the same thought but didn't like the idea. Tellus entered the stable to find the owner, and Pen followed.

The owner of the stable was the wife of the innkeeper. She was tall, with grayish green hair tied back in a tight bun. The stable boy was rubbing down Phobos. There was a little girl as well, playing with whatever she could get her hands on. Her hair was pale like the boy's but with a few green highlights.

"If you want a room, you'll have to talk to Danaus inside," the woman said, writing notes in a small book. Her stylus was a thin piece of charcoal that stained her fingers.

"I'd like to sell one of our horses first," Tellus said, pleasantly enough.

She stopped writing and eyed him. "Zagus, stop." The boy stopped brushing Phobos, looking confused. "You even got money for a room?"

"Sadly, no, we were robbed on the way here."

"Mm-hm." She seemed irritated.

"Which was why I was hoping for a trade." Tellus's voice was a little more strained.

She crossed her arms. "I should kick you out. We don't need any horses."

"Sell it for a profit then," Tellus suggested.

The woman sighed, looked at Tellus, then at Pen, and then the horses. Zagus still stood with the brush in hand, watching them.

"The brown one, ten silvers," she offered.

"He is the sturdier of the two, but I need him for our travels," Tellus countered. "How about the pale one for nine coins?"

She sucked her teeth. "Seven for that one."

Pen cleared her throat. "Sorry, but my father was a rancher, and I know Demos is worth at least eighteen silvers. Given that you want a bargain, of course, how about fifteen?"

The woman sucked her teeth again, an annoying habit. "Ten."

"Fourteen?"

"Eleven."

Pen didn't want to push it. This woman was agitated to begin with, and asking for more might get them turned away. She was going to get some back for the room anyway. "Fine, eleven."

The woman counted the coins from a purse tied inside a fold of her skirt and handed them to Tellus without another word. Zagus went back to brushing Phobos.

They went into the inn and bought a room and food for the night. After picking a table to eat, Tellus said, "So your father was a rancher?"

"No, he was a mercenary," Pen replied.

"He taught you how to fight then?"

"Mm-hm. He wanted to make sure his only daughter could defend herself."

Their training sessions had started when Pen was young, practicing with swords, knives, axes, even staves for two hours a day. They traveled around a lot, working for hire mostly. Once, when her father left her in a village to carry out a job as a hired guard for a merchant for a month, she had kept up with her training. The boys made fun of her until one of them provoked her into a fight. He had kept pinching her arse, saying that he only wanted her to dance. She knocked his front teeth out and they left her alone. When her father returned the boy's mother turned to him and demanded that Pen be punished. Her father listened to the whole story twice, once from the boy then from Pen herself. The boy had admitted to pinching her "once or twice" and her father laughed at him. They left the village the next day telling Pen he was glad she fought back, but that her reaction was a little extreme.

He'd died a few years later from an infected wound. Pen always believed her father would go down fighting like a warrior, but all it took was a rusty nail in his foot. She traveled alone for a long time, doing odd jobs like her father had.

Tellus paused with his flagon partway to his lips. "Then how did you know how much Demos was worth?"

"I didn't." She smirked. "But I've sold horses before."

Tellus put the flagon down, angry. In a lower voice, he asked, "Did you cheat her?"

Pen stopped eating the beef stew, "I don't know, but would you rather have slept in the streets?"

Tellus didn't reply, but he didn't look impressed. Pen continued eating. The food was pretty good.

Once the meal was finished, Tellus sat back, enjoying the ale. Pen was watching the fire dance, her own flagon in hand, listening to a bard sing about the Ichorian War. These city-states could never decide on anything together, which often led to small wars between two or three, but the Ichorian War happened when two of the biggest cities, Stymphalia and Kalymnos, forced their neighbors to fight with them for control of Ichorisis itself. The war was a failure on both sides, leading to a peace treaty but thousands dead.

"—some work."

Pen snapped out of her daze, tearing her eyes away from the fire. "Hm?"

"I said we might need more coin. The ferry across the river will be expensive, and it's good to have extra as backup. We'll need to find some quick work."

Being a nomad originally gave her the skills to live on her own and gather information. Over the past few months of practicing her power, and staying in hiding, she refined those skills again. One of the best ways to acquire money was to talk to someone who heard a lot of talk about the town. That, or look for wanted posters.

Pen stood and headed over to Danaus the innkeeper. He was wiping down the wooden bar top with a rag. A man in a dirty white tunic under a brown vest was already passed out on the bar. Danaus was about to wake him before Pen got his attention.

Hopping onto a stool and leaning forward on her arms, she asked, "Where can someone get a little work around here?"

He looked her up and down quickly, as she knew he would. She wasn't overly pretty, so she wanted to get that out of the way. She had no intentions of whoring herself out, but when men realized there wasn't much to show, they tended to leave that idea alone.

Danaus leaned on his hands on the other side of the counter. "Could stay here if ya like, could always use another barmaid." He smiled.

Well, it usually worked.

"Something for the both of us would be nice." Tellus stepped from behind her. "We need to be on our way in a couple days, so something temporary."

Danaus eyed Tellus, not appreciating the interruption. Pen was glad for it. She smiled at Tellus and leaned a little closer to him, acting familiar. She watched the greasy look in Danaus's eyes die; he thought they were married. He didn't need to know otherwise.

"I hear the docks are looking for workers to bring merchandise into town," he suggested. "Also, the blacksmith is looking for a new right hand man, if you're good with numbers."

"That sounds promising, thank you." Tellus put a hand on Pen's shoulder, guiding her back to their table.

"What in the bloody name of Nyx was that about?" Tellus demanded once they sat.

"Looking for work, like you said," she answered, not bothering to keep the frustration out of her voice; she thought she'd been helping.

"We need to keep a low profile."

"I'm pretty sure asking for work isn't going to expose us. Expose us to what? No one knows where we're going. Most of the people probably aren't even aware of the curse yet, anyway."

"People *have* noticed that no one is dying. Trust me, I've heard stories, and there were probably one hundred people at your own execution. Some are calling it the Era of Undying," Tellus said. "Some may want to stop us once they realize we're trying to end it. They see it as a blessing from the damn gods. Besides, you want to keep your identity quiet, right? Because of what you can do? That doesn't entail talking to random people who might remember your face."

"How do you suggest we find work then?"

"The wanted posters for an easy bounty."

Damn.

The next morning Pen and Tellus went down to the main gate where the wanted posters hung. Most of them were crudely drawn portraits of criminals wanted for murder, maiming, or extensive thievery. One man was wanted for digging up the dead and robbing them. The square was bustling with life, and the smell of horses and oxen filled the air. They were everywhere, bringing in goods and food for the city. Two men standing beside a donkey cart filled with barley argued over something. Pen couldn't tell what they were arguing about, but it looked like the bald man won; the other threw up his hands and walked away.

Tellus indicated a drawing at the edge of the board. "How about this one?"

It depicted a man named Tangaes, who had last been seen within the city only a couple of days ago. The bounty was small but a good return; he was only wanted for robbing a jeweler. He looked young, and based on the dates, he robbed the jeweler only a week ago. He was probably still hiding in the city, scared.

"Sounds easy enough," Pen agreed, "But what about that one?"

Pen pointed to a poster that depicted a middle ages man with thick hair and beard. He was rather average looking but the description below stated he had a bird tattooed on his hand. The poster also said that his name was unknown but he was a possible gang leader and wanted murderer.

"The price is higher," Tellus said, "but more complicated then we need."

"I would be more challenging though, could be fun."

Tellus looked to Pen slightly confused, as if she had said something odd. "Do you enjoy hunting people?"

"What?! No, well bring people who think they are important down is entertaining. But, I don't like hurting them. The smaller thief would be faster anyway, we should start with the jeweler."

"Talking to other merchants in the area will help too," Tellus said, taking down the poster of Tangaes. "He has to be living here somewhere."

"I could start with the jeweler, then. You ask the others?" Pen suggested. "Cover more ground that way."

"I may have let you out of the chains, but I'm not letting you out of my sight. King Aegeus still considers you a fugitive." At least he had the decency to lower his voice.

"It would be quicker if we split up," Pen argued.

"No."

Pen grimaced but followed.

The jeweler didn't know anything other than which way the thief ran before he vanished. He'd stolen a single ruby before the owner saw him, but it was the size of a robin's egg. The information was enough to tell Pen he probably knew the lay of the land and its hiding places if he got away so quickly.

The merchants around the area didn't recognize the man when Tellus showed them the drawing, and neither did the other jewelers or bankers, so the thief hadn't yet sold his prize.

By midday they still had no leads. They stopped at a booth for a stick of fried fish.

"We should head to the gates next," Tellus suggested. "Maybe someone saw him leave."

"The poster *is* a few days old," Pen said. "I could check out the docks while you do that."

Tellus sighed. "Again, no."

After they finished the fish, Tellus headed to the gates. The poster was folded in his belt, not hidden. Pen lifted the parchment from him and melted into the crowd. Tellus hadn't noticed her disappearance. He was a captain of the guard, so he was probably good with faces and describing them, so he didn't need the poster. She pocketed it and headed to the docks.

The docks were more crowded than the square. People bustled everywhere amongst the stink of fish. The docks themselves were relatively small for a city, but giant cargo ships couldn't travel the river waters. The docks were full of smaller barges. Seagulls filled the sky, and their droppings covered the ground, along with mud and fish guts.

Pen might have left Tellus behind, but she kept his advice about laying low. She kept her hood up to hide her hair. These river people were light skinned, with dark, almost black hair. Her purple hair would be noticeable.

"Ya, I know him," one sailor said, after she'd flagged down two dozen others.

"Do you know where he is?"

"What's he wanted for?" the sailor asked; he obviously couldn't read.

"Nothing, it's a drawing from his uncle who hasn't been feeling well. He hired me to find his nephew," Pen lied.

"Ah, Tangaes lives on Copper Street in the flat painted blue, second floor, I think. Didn't know he had an uncle. He never mentioned one."

"They didn't get along well, long story, involved a kitchen maid. Now that he's sick, he'd like to make amends and see Tangaes one more time."

The sailor smiled, like he knew a special secret. "He needn't worry 'bout that, miss. He'll be fine."

"What makes you say that?" Her nerves prickled.

"'Tis the Era of Undying, miss. It's good he wants to reunite with Tangaes. He doesn't have much family, but there's no rush."

He gave a small bow then went on his way.

Anticipation got her blood moving again; she finally had a lead. Tellus would be angry at her leaving, but it had worked out. She should find him and tell him her findings before going to Tangaes' flat. This was rather fun.

She headed back to Black Waters, planning to wait for Tellus there, but he was already at the door of the inn, talking to Danaus and his wife. He did not look happy.

"If you see her, get a guard or messenger to find me," he ordered. "I'll be at the Tall Keep."

"Honey! There you are." Pen called. She hugged Tellus, acting innocent. "Sorry about losing you. I'll admit I got distracted by the bakery, then I lost you in the crowd.

Took longer than I thought to find this place, but the baker was kind enough to point me this way."

Tellus just stared, trying to hide his fury. Danaus and his wife looked relieved. Tellus must have frightened them a bit with his military demeanor.

"I'm just glad you're safe, *honey*." It would have been endearing if the words weren't so clipped. "Come inside, we have to talk."

Leaving the innkeeper and his wife looking worried, Tellus led her to their room. He locked the door, then turned on her.

"What, in the bloody name of Nyx, were you doing?!"

Pen had known he would be angry, but his restraint was impressive. He looked almost ready to break the wall.

"I found us a lead," she answered calmly. "The thief lives on Copper Street."

The wind was taken from his sails a bit, but he was still livid.

"You went to the docks?" He sounded astonished.

Pen smirked. "You thought I'd run off, didn't you?"

"Of course I did! You're a fugitive put in my charge by the king. And I can't do my bloody job if you escape." Why was there hurt in his eyes?

"Why are you taking this personally?" she asked. "I was helping."

"Because my friend is dying!"

Pen was taken aback by the outburst. He'd said "friend," not "king."

Tellus took a breath to calm himself. "My best friend wants to die, and I can't do my last duty for him if you keep running off."

He honestly cared for the man, not as his king but as his friend. Pen understood his anger now; she would have done anything for Arch.

"Fine. Next time I'll let you know, but will you at least heed my advice rather than ignore me?"

"I didn't ignore you. We talked to the jeweler, and I had every intention of going to the docks. It was a good idea. You were too rash to follow my lead."

"I'm not one of your soldiers," she snapped. He was right, though.

"No, but you are my captive, and I can easily set my own bounty on your head or keep you locked up for a long time. I could go to the Acheron myself."

The threat of imprisonment made her pause. She'd never see her family again, and he was within his rights to do just that. She wanted to reach the Acheron as much as he did, so he knew where she'd go if she ran, she had nowhere else. Still, she had no intention of being chained up again.

"Fine, I'll follow your lead, but on one condition."

"Which is?"

"Once this is over, and people can die again, you drop the charges against me."

Tellus blanched. "I can't do that."

"You're captain of the Stymphalian Guard. Of course you can."

"Not without the king's order."

"Then send a letter now, because it won't reach him once we've fixed death."

Tellus was quiet for a moment. "Very well. Once we've collected the bounty I'll hire a courier to send him a message directly. I can't guarantee anything Aegeus may or may not do, but I can try."

It would have to be enough for now; she could always run once they found Nyx. Arch and Alard would understand. "Then we have an agreement."

Tellus ran a hand through his green hair. "So you found him on Copper Street?"

Pen took a seat in the only chair, tossing the poster on the small table. "I haven't found him yet. I learned where he was, then came here to make a plan with you."

Copper Street was deserted at this time of night. There were no taverns in this neighborhood, only residential homes. The wealth didn't stretch as far as the outer ring of the city. Some windows were boarded up and the streets were grimy. The houses had been painted when constructed, but the paint was now dull and chipped. There were only three buildings painted blue. One was only a single floor that appeared to be a garden roof. One of the two storey buildings was boarded up. That left only one. There was a dull flicker of light from the dirty glass on the second floor.

Pen was the one to suggest they come at night, though Tellus wanted to take the direct approach. He assumed a thief could have honor and come quietly. There was always the chance he might, but if he didn't they could shut him up easily enough. The wanted poster hadn't said he was needed alive. They couldn't kill him, but unconscious would work fine.

There was a narrow flight of stairs leading up to the door on the side. They made more noise than she would have liked, given the stealthy approach, but there were no other exits out of this flat. Tellus had circled it before as Pen kept watch on the dirty window and door.

Tellus knocked. "Tangaes? We'd like to have a word if you don't mind. Please be civil and open the door."

Silence came from inside, but through the gap in the door frame Pen saw a light flicker out.

"Come now, son, we only want to talk."

Nothing.

Tellus tried the door; of course it was locked. He grunted in frustration. Dropping the civil approach, he took a step back to ram the door.

Pen stopped him mid-step and whispered, "Prick my finger."

"What?"

"My hand healed after the robber on the road, and I don't have any of my own weapons." She didn't mention her hidden razor, but Tellus didn't need to know of that yet. "Cut my finger."

"So you can perform your blood magic?" he accused.

"Obviously."

Tellus paused for a moment, considering his options. "You will only open the door."

With a mock salute, Pen said, "Yes, sir."

He sighed but took his dagger in one hand and Pen's hand in the other. He slid the metal quickly over the pad of her forefinger. It twitched from the sting, but Pen was used to it.

Drawing out a tendril, Pen slid it into the keyhole and unlocked the door. It slid open a bit on its own.

She wiped her blood clean and melted it back into her finger. Stepping back and smiling, she offered Tellus entrance first. A vein in his neck twitched, but he stepped inside.

The flat was tiny, and they were right about the lack of other exits. There was only the one door and window. A bed took up one whole side, and an uneven table sat by the window with a smoking, unlit candle.

A slight man stood in the far corner, facing them with a knife. It was dark, but Pen could see his hand shaking.

"Relax, son." Tellus's voice was soft now. "I know this is frightening, having strangers barge into your room, but we're not here to hurt you."

He stepped toward the shaking figure, one hand extended in peace, the other hovering over his concealed dagger. Pen slid to the table and lit the candle with the near empty tinder box.

The candle didn't light the room perfectly, but it would have to do. The figure in the corner was a thin youth, no more than seventeen maybe, with brown hair and narrow eyes. He matched the image of the poster perfectly. The shaking knife was gripped in both hands now, he wasn't an experienced fighter.

"You're Tangaes, then?" Tellus asked.

"Aye, and I-I have the money, I swear," Tangaes stammered. "W-well not coin exactly, but I can pay."

"With what then?" Pen asked, playing along.

"I took a ruby," he admitted. "It's in the bed."

Pen crossed the room to the bed. Disappointed that he had given in so easily, she found a slit in the straw mattress. Tellus kept an eye on Tangaes as Pen found a little pouch. Inside was the large ruby, just as he'd said. She pocketed it. Something was wrong, though. He was a coward, clearly, but he was too generous with his guilt. He hadn't even tried to deny the charge.

"That's enough, right? Right? To cover my payment?" Tangaes insisted. There was terrified hope in his eyes, staring at Pen.

"Payment for what?" Tellus asked. He must have sensed the same wrongness. Tangaes was talking about something else.

"For my debt," he clarified, confused. He turned back to Tellus, "S—so there's no need to break my knees, right?"

"We weren't going to break anything, only take you to the Tall Keep to answer for the robbery." Tellus still watched Tangaes closely, but the news just confused the youth.

"You're n-not one of Vox's men?"

"No."

Tangaes was on the verge of tears now. He slumped against the wall, and his arms dropped like the knife was too heavy. Tellus took the knife and put it on the table.

"We can help you, Tangaes," Tellus said.

Tangaes blinked a couple of times as hoped dawned again. "You're with the Ragged Wolves then?"

Before Tellus could deny it, Pen answered, "Yes."

Tellus shot her a look, but she shrugged. This was getting more interesting.

"You got my message then." Tangaes straightened and pushed away from the wall. "You can kill Vox."

"Maybe, but why would we?" Pen inquired.

"You can keep the ruby and take me to the Tall Keep, whatever you want. Just kill Vox and erase my debt."

"Where can Vox be found?" she asked.

"I don't know exactly, but he does a lot of work through Xestir tavern. That's where I met him."

"Has he wronged you?" Tellus asked.

Tangaes turned to him again, confused. "I thought the Ragged Wolves didn't care about details."

"Slight change in business strategy. We like to know what we're getting into," Pen said. She wanted to hit Tellus.

"He loaned me coin to use at the inn. I was on a winning streak but lost it all in one bad hand of Conquest. Bad luck, you know, but I could get it back. He was there and knew I had potential. He let me keep playing as long as I paid him back with interest. And I was stupid enough to agree. I've paid him back the original loan, but the interest keeps going up. I've given him everything, but he won't leave me alone, saying the interest hasn't been paid, and that it's rising because of that. He said if I didn't pay by the full moon he'd send someone to take out my knee, then the next one a week later." He was nearly crying again.

"This isn't really—"

"Our usual way of business, but we'll take care of him," Pen interrupted.

Tellus glared at her.

She believed Tangaes's story. He was a poor commoner with a gambling habit. Not a habit she wanted to encourage, but she hated loan sharks and gang leaders. Her father had been involved with one when she was young. There was only one way out of that situation, and her father had gotten lucky in that duel.

She had also seen a wanted poster with Vox's name and description earlier, when Tellus had picked Tangaes. There was no drawing of Vox, but the bounty was much larger.

"We're still taking you to the Keep," Tellus said. "Will you come willingly?"

"Yes, yes whatever you need," Tangaes agreed gratefully. "I'll probably be safer from Vox's goons there."

Tellus took Tangaes by the arm and led him to the door. Neither Tellus nor Pen mentioned that the city guards might take one of his hands for the thievery. Pen picked up the knife from the table.

"You have a sheath for this?"

"No." He probably couldn't afford one.

"Mind if I keep it?" she asked. "As payment for the Wolves."

"Oh, well… yes, of course."

Pen stuck it in her belt, mindful of its sharp edge.

They took one of the main roads heading directly to the Tall Keep. The city roads were laid out like spokes on a wheel. These main roads were safe enough, but the smaller alleys connecting them were better left untraveled at night.

At the Tall Keep, Tellus handed Tangaes over to the guard on duty, then turned to Pen.

He held out a hand. "Ruby."

She took it from her pocket and handed it over. Ever the honorable man. He then asked the men on duty for parchment and had them send a letter to King Aegeus about her freedom. Pen was thankful that he did though she stayed quiet.

Tellus gave it to the guard, who then counted out their bounty. Fresh coin in hand, they headed back to the Black Waters inn. Neither spoke on the walk.

Once in their room, after paying for a second night, it was Tellus who started the conversation.

"What makes you think we should find this Vox?" he asked. "He just sounds like a low-life loan shark."

"He probably is. You heard Tangaes, he said men were being sent after him. Which means Vox is their leader, and he's running a crime syndicate."

"Yes, but why should *we* go after him?"

"You saw the reward. It has to be ten times the amount for Tangaes," she argued.

"We have enough money now. We should leave this alone."

"We'd be doing this city a great favor," she said, "taking out one of their crime lords."

Tellus was quiet for a moment. "We had a man like that in Stymphalia a few years back. Terrorizing the people and even taking limbs as payment."

"So you agree with me?"

"Not exactly; this city's crime is not our business. And I don't want to get involved with those 'Ragged Wolves,' whatever they are."

"Probably another gang."

"So we'd be helping the reputation of one syndicate while harming another."

"At least we'd be harming one and helping Tangaes. We owe him something, don't we? They're going to take his hand for the ruby."

"I don't like the fate of that boy either, but it's no longer our business."

He wasn't going to let that go, so Pen let the argument drop.

Chapter Nine

They were leaving in the morning on Tellus's order, but Pen lay awake in the only bed, thinking of Tangaes and her father.

Her mother had died in childbirth, so her father had been left alone to take care of her. They got by fine, but when Pen was ten her father had borrowed money to pay for food during one harsh winter when he couldn't find work.

The same problem of interest plagued them after Father paid the loan shark. It went as far as the leader of the gang offering to erase Father's debts if he handed over his daughter. That snapped the final thread, and Father challenged the leader to a duel. He accepted, expecting an easy fight.

Her father, being a mercenary fighter, took him down. He nearly lost an eye, but after he killed their leader, the gang left him alone. The next day Pen and her father gathered everything and moved on.

Tellus was sleeping on the floor beneath the window. Watching him, Pen got up, threw on her cloak, and took his handkerchief. Making sure the knife was in place, she crept out the door and headed for Xestir tavern.

It was well past midnight now, but stragglers still walked in this area. The residence of Copper Street was quiet, but Xestir tavern was bustling with business. She knew it was a long shot, but she went in and took a seat at the bar. After ordering an ale, she turned on her stool to watch the crowd.

Xestir was larger than Black Waters because it didn't bother running an inn. The place was lit by torches as well as a fireplace, and several groups played Conquest. The air was thick with smoke from the fires and haze from tobacco leaves.

Pen remembered from the wanted poster that Vox had a tattoo of a black bird on his left hand. She scanned the people, watching their hands. Men played and laughed too loudly. Some women played among them. There were young women, either sitting on the lap of one man or flirting between a couple of patrons.

Pen nursed the single ale for two hours; for a different angle she'd changed seats from the bar to the back of the room beside the fire, but there was no sign of Vox. She downed the rest of the sour ale and stood to leave. Tellus was right, Tangaes would have to fend for himself.

A table of six men erupted, drawing Pen's eye as she passed. One man was not joining in the joyful rumble; he was slumped in his seat, staring at the cards as if they'd personally betrayed him. A woman with light blue hair falling past her shoulders was perched on the lap of another man. His hair was dark, with a straggly beard like the rest of the common folk here. He lifted a hand to the woman's ear and whispered. It was his left hand. Pen stopped mid-stride as she spotted the bird tattoo. The woman gave a false smile and trailed a hand down the man's stomach to his trousers. He told her one more thing, then pushed her off to stand. He indicated one of the closed doors on the second floor. The woman climbed the stairs, heading to the room as the man stepped through a back door that led outside. Pen followed him.

He headed to the alley between Xestir and the neighboring building. It was dark, but Pen watched his profile as he started pissing on the building and into the gutter. Pen opened the scab on her finger that Tellus had cut before.

This would have to be fast.

"Excuse me, are you Vox?" she asked, sweetly approaching him.

His eyes snapped to attention, angry at being caught with his trousers down. "Who the hell are you?"

She shot blood at him, wrapping it around his head, pinning his mouth closed. Her knife from Tangaes pressed against his throat now.

"Are you?" she hissed.

Wide eyed as a deer, he nodded.

"Good. Fix your pants." She wouldn't have to maim an innocent man.

Once his trousers were finally laces again she forced him down on his knees. He tried to pull away from the knife, but more blood trapped his legs on the ground.

She sent two new tendrils to pin his hands. Tightened the blood on his wrists, making them thin blades at the same time, she cut through the bone. He screamed as his hands were removed. The scream turned into a gag as her blood filled his mouth. In the same manner as his hands, she took his tongue.

He choked and spat his own blood now, holding his arms to his chest.

Kneeling next to him, she gathered the tongue in the handkerchief and picked up the hands.

"Any debt you hold over anyone in this city has been erased," she told him softly. "Understood?"

He didn't respond at first but stared in cold rage and pain.

She touched the cold steel to his throat again.

"Understood?"

He nodded, coughing more blood.

"Good." She withdrew the rest of her blood, wiped it on his tunic, and left him kneeling in the alley.

Chapter Ten

The next morning was quiet. Pen and Tellus enjoyed the breakfast of porridge and bread provided by Danaus. Pen hadn't told Tellus about Vox. Shortly after meeting him in the alley she'd wrapped his tongue in Tellus's handkerchief then she handed it over to the men stationed at the Tall Keep, along with the hands, the tattoo acting as proof that Vox had been taken care of. She told the city guard where she'd left him, and some were dispatched to take him to a cell. It was enough for Pen to receive the generous bounty. She kept the coin hidden on her person, intending to get a new handkerchief for Tellus. He'd probably think he'd lost the old one.

After breaking their fast, they left Phobos at the stables a little while longer. They headed down to the docks and booked passage on a barge large enough to hold several horses. Fortunately, it was leaving soon and the sailor was willing to wait an hour. They went back to Black Waters stable.

Danaus's wife was there, and Zagus led out Phobos. Tellus thanked the boy and gave him a coin.

"Excuse me," Pen said to Danaus's wife, "one more thing."

Pen took out thirteen coins and handed them to her. She looked between the coins to Pen, as if wondering whether one or both might bite.

"They're for Demos, plus a little profit."

"Thought you hardly had enough coin to pay for the room."

Pen shrugged. "I got lucky last night."

The woman snapped her fingers at Zagus, who scurried off and returned with Demos. Pen rubbed his neck, feeling the warmth and strength of the beast. Zagus had taken care of him well. Pen tossed him a tip.

Tellus watched her, not hiding the suspicion as she left the stable with Demos. "Where did you get that coin?"

"I couldn't sleep last night, so I went to the tavern and played some hands of Conquest. They were some good hands." Her smile showed equal parts innocence and malice.

Tellus started down the road back to the docks, Phobos's reins in hand. "They were certainly loud enough last night, must have been fun."

Pen followed through with the lie. "It was, but one man was a bit upset at losing, so he smashed his tankard. He was thrown out quickly enough."

The barge was waiting for them, as promised. It took some time getting the skittish horses on board, but once Phobos and Demos were secured on the deck below, they were off. The river wasn't huge by any means; the shore could easily be seen, but it was the widest section before it opened into the lake.

A couple of hours passed with Pen standing at the bow, enjoying the spray of the water, while Tellus chatted with the sailors. When the captain of the barge asked where they were headed, Tellus said they were seeing the country. Given how simple but effective the ruse had been at Black Waters, they continued to travel under the guise of husband and wife. It felt wrong to Pen, like she was betraying Arch, but it was easier to travel.

Once they docked at the south shore, it was almost midday. Phobos and Demos were recovered and appreciated the solid ground. Pen thanked the sailors and was about to mount Demos when the captain approached Tellus.

Tellus paused beside Phobos. The captain probably had one more thing to say. Another sailor came up behind Tellus. Before Pen could utter anything the sailor clubbed Tellus on the back of the head with the hilt of his dagger.

"Hey—" A hand clamped over Pen's mouth.

She bit down hard, tasting blood. Another man joined the first and pinned her hands behind her. A bag was shoved over her head, cutting off the noonday sun. Pain erupted over her left ear, and she blacked out.

She couldn't tell if it was day anymore. Everything was dark and cold. She cursed herself over and over about not fighting back enough. The cut on her finger was still there; she could have taken them all out. That was probably an overstatement, but it would have been enough to run, at least. She could use her blood now to remove the bag over her head, but the noise around her made her hesitate.

It was quiet, but there was the crackle of fire and footsteps. The voices were either hushed or in the distance.

Footfalls grew closer to her. She lay still, bound and blind again, waiting to strike. She kept her eyes closed, for no other reason than she couldn't see with the bag on anyway. It worked out, in a way. The bag was ripped off her head. Her head hit the floor again, causing red light to flash across her eyelids, but she pretended to be unconscious to bide her time. She didn't move.

Whoever had removed the bag watched her; she could feel it.

There was a chuckle. "Nice try."

Several hands lifted her. Her eyes snapped open involuntarily at the sudden movement. She couldn't get a good look at him, but a man dragged her through a twisting rock corridor. They entered a large cave and he deposited her in front of a large, well made stone pit in the center of the room, filling it with light and warmth.

She found herself in a cave refurbished into some kind of reception area. The central fire cast light on the raw stone walls, ceiling, and a single large banner of a dark blue background with the black stitching of a wolf's face.

There were fewer than a dozen people in the cavern, a mix of men and women. All were clad in armor that had clearly been used many times before. One woman stood at the fire pit opposite Pen. She was tall, not beefy like a man, but thick. Her red hair was chopped short enough to just pass her ears. There was a scar cutting down the right side of her face. It ran from her temple, pulling down her mouth. That side of her face constantly frowned, despite the fact that she was grinning at Pen like they were old friends.

There was a grunt, then the sound of something being dragged. Pen watched, growing sick as Tellus was dumped beside her, still unconscious. The man who dragged him in was bald and missing several teeth. The bald man took a bucket from a comrade wearing a dented breastplate, and threw the water at Tellus.

Tellus woke, gasping from the shock, coughing up the liquid.

"Palrig," the red haired woman said in a monotone, "was that the last bucket of fresh water? That was for the animals."

"It wasn't water." Bald Palrig gave a smug smile.

Pen smelled piss.

Tellus got to his knees, spitting with his hair stuck to his face.

"Who are you?" Tellus demanded, ever the commander.

"I'm Raisa," she replied, "leader of the Ragged Wolves."

Pen's heart dropped into the dirt.

"Although you should know that, given that you are one of us." She smiled in a friendly way. "Even took one of our jobs."

"You're bounty hunters?" Tellus nearly scoffed. "This is about that boy, Tangaes?"

"No. Well, yes, I suppose. He sent us the request, which you so graciously took care of for us."

Tellus looked to Pen as the pieces fitted together in his mind. If he could have killed her with his eyes alone, he would have. "What did you do?"

Pen couldn't meet his eyes. Every nerve was jumping, telling her to run, but she couldn't kill them. Even if she did knock them out, like the bandits, she didn't know the way out of the caves.

"It was rather impressive, actually." Raisa strode around the fire and knelt beside Pen. "Taking a man's tongue so he couldn't talk is one thing, but his hands as well? Was that a precaution in case he could write?"

Pen didn't respond, though she refused to look away from Raisa. She might be scared, but she refused to let this woman see that. It kept her from looking at Tellus as well. He was no doubt disgusted.

"I took his hand with the tattoo as proof of who he was. I'll admit I can't lift a full grown man."

"But both hands?"

"In case he *could* write."

"How did you bring him down in the first place?"

Pen shrugged it off. "I caught him with his trousers down."

Raisa laughed. It was more than a little unnerving, since only half of her face moved. Pen's heart panicked like a cornered deer, but she kept her face blank.

Tellus's glare turned to Raisa as she came around to his side.

"You honestly had no idea where she went last night?" Raisa asked him.

He stayed quiet for now.

"Oh," she mocked, "not very good relations with your wife."

"She's not my wife."

"Too bad, you two seemed cute together." Raisa stood in front of the fire now, facing them both. "Now, I'm a reasonable person, but when it comes to this business and my family, I take it seriously."

"You can take the bounty we have from Vox then," Tellus said.

"We're not bounty hunters," she snapped. "We are assassins, and Tangaes sent us the job of Vox, which you stole. The coin would be nice, obviously, we are taking that, but you damaged our reputation." She turned to Pen again. "While what you did was impressive, it wasn't exactly… elegant."

Tellus scoffed now. "Assassins being elegant?"

"We may be killers, but we have standards," she countered. "She made a show of it. Why not just kill him?"

Pen stayed quiet, not sure what to say. She stole a glance at Tellus, but there was no indication of anything. She thought a partial truth would work.

"When I was ten, my father borrowed from a man like him to buy food. The man offered to take me instead of the money. My father killed him."

"Okay, but why not kill Vox, if it worked out well last time?"

"I wanted him to suffer."

"Hm." Raisa grew quiet. "Yiga, go get Narciso."

A thin woman with short blond hair looked surprised but left the chamber. Raisa waited until Yiga came back, supporting another man. Raisa took a rickety chair and put it by the fire. Raisa and Yiga helped the man into the seat.

The smell was almost enough to make Pen retch. The man only wore trousers, exposing his torso. There was a gash across his stomach that had been stitched closed, but the flesh was dead and rotting. Narciso was clearly in pain, his light brown hair stuck to his face with sweat from fever. He leaned back, but Yiga kept an arm over his shoulder; it looked like he wanted to pass out.

"He was disemboweled last week," Raisa explained. "It was a routine job, just a priest stealing from the temple coffers who liked children a little too much. One of the children's parents sent us the request. The priest got lucky with a hidden knife and gutted him, leaving him in a mess of his own intestines. Yiga found the priest and shortly took his head. The priest wasn't dead, so we kept the head. The eyes keep blinking and watching us; that spark of life is still there, but it can't talk or breathe. Something is wrong, and I thought you might have some ideas?"

Pen couldn't look away from Narciso's stitched gut. He probably couldn't eat anything.

"Narciso?" Tellus said. He looked shocked. "Narciso, look at me, please."

Narciso was staring in the distance, but he focused on Tellus. Even that effort seemed to hurt.

"Captain?" he croaked.

"By the gods, we thought you were dead," Tellus exclaimed.

Narciso sighed a laugh. "Wish I was at this point."

"Well, this is different." Raisa crossed her arms and let them talk.

"What happened after the ambush in the mountains?" Tellus asked.

"I was lost after that avalanche, but these people found me… said I could join them."

"So you murder for money now?"

"It's not like that!" he said, offended by Tellus's disappointment. "We investigate them and see if the world would be safer."

He was cut off by pain, nearly doubling over.

"Narciso is right, we don't kill everyone," Raisa interjected. "If we did, there would be a lot of dead fathers from greedy children, or husbands from wives already cheating on them. Vox was one of those people we're taken care of before." She always said 'take care of' like she was doing a service. "But with this botchery," she indicated Pen, "people may think we *are* ruthless and bloodthirsty. So since you did one job fairly, if not cleanly, you will work for us to pay us back."

Tellus blanched. "What? You're already taking our money, why force us to help you?"

"We're not taking all of your money, only what you owe us for Vox. We could take your tongues for silence, hands too if you can write," she smirked at Pen, "but I like you. So you repay us in one job, and you go free. Off to travel the country or where ever you were going. The only worthwhile place south of here is the Acheron."

Pen couldn't reply, but she kept her jaw set. As long as they let her go to her son, she'd do any job. She didn't want to, but they weren't giving many options.

"Why should we believe you?" Tellus asked. "Why not have us killed?"

"Because people can't die, though we could keep your head, like that priest." She grew quiet, possibly considering the idea. "But we don't kill innocents, or maim them, unless you give us reason to believe otherwise, then things will change. Unbind them."

Palrig knelt and cut Tellus's bonds, then Pen's. Tellus stood, pushing hair out of his eyes.

"I am sorry about that bucket," Raisa admitted. "I thought he'd just hit you."

"So what's this job?" Tellus asked, ignoring the comment.

"Simple enough. A merchant who works with spices. He's cheating his customers and business partners. It was actually one of his partners in Stymphalia who sent us the message."

"You have a branch in Stymphalia?" He had no idea of this.

"Spies mainly as couriers, but yes, Captain. You're from there, I take it?"

Tellus grunted, angry that he'd given that away, although his conversation with Narciso gave a good hint. "I am."

"Captain Tellus from Stymphalia," Raisa said, tasting the words. "And where are you from, Pen?"

Pen hadn't realized this woman knew her name. But the sailors from the barge had worked for Raisa, and Pen hadn't used a fake name.

"Malliae," she said, instantly kicking herself for not making something up.

"Where's that?" Raisa asked.

"Tiny village in the west."

"Why unbind us?" Tellus asked, still testing the situation.

"A matter of trust. You're free to carry out the job however you like. But you won't leave until it's complete. If you try to run, we will stop you."

"You can't kill us."

"But we can take your foot."

Tellus fell silent, glaring, then asked, "This merchant, where is he?"

"The small town west of here. All we have to do is follow the river."

"Fine, we'll do it," Pen said. It seemed easy enough that they'd be back on their way to the Acheron soon.

"Good." Raisa smiled. "But I want you to do it." She indicated Tellus.

"Why me specifically?" Tellus asked, horrified. "I won't harm someone for coin."

"The coin is for us," Raisa admitted.

"I won't."

"Then we take your foot now."

Raisa watched him as if there was no argument. Tellus looked as though he wanted to push her into the fire, but he didn't say anything.

"The priest," Pen said, breaking the tension, "you said you still have his head?"

Raisa turned to her quizzically. "Yes, why?"

"When it was taken off, did the body try to get it back?"

"No, it just lay limp."

"The blood didn't try to connect it back?" Tellus asked, appearing to appreciate the distraction.

"No, why would it?"

Pen faltered, but Tellus covered for her.

"You're right that people can't die. We heard similar stories but wanted to know what happened in this situation."

"Can we see the head?" Pen asked.

Raisa shrugged. "Don't see why not. Palrig, you mind?"

Palrig left through a natural archway. Narciso stood with Yiga's help, grunting.

"You shouldn't move much," Raisa said, concerned. "You can stay, the fire is warm."

"I don't want to see that thing," Narciso said, no doubt meaning the head.

Raisa let him go.

Palrig returned with a brown canvas sack. He handed it to Raisa, who reached in and pulled out the head. Pen took an involuntary step back. Tellus looked equally disgusted and horrified. It was the head of a sixty year old man with gray hair. Raisa held it by that hair as it watched them with a gaping mouth. The blue eyes twitched between Tellus and Pen.

"Why keep it?" Tellus asked. It sounded like he was concerned for the priest.

"I want to make sure he stays dead or at least can't hurt anyone again," Raisa explained, "and given what you told me about the bodies, it was a good idea."

"Can he feel pain?" Pen asked. Being held by the hair like that always hurt.

"No idea. Maybe." Raisa put it back in the sack and handed it back to Palrig.

"Leave us, but Palrig, you and Daeson stay by the archway," Raisa ordered.

Everyone left through the only archway. Once they were relatively alone, Raisa appeared to grow worried. Pen couldn't pinpoint why, given the demeanor of the woman before. She could no doubt hold her own in a fight, that scar was probably proof, and there were two others close by so she wasn't outnumbered.

Pen's nerves still hummed at even a snap in the fire, but she forced most of her fear to subside. Raisa seemed like a woman of her word, and once this merchant was out of the way she and Tellus would be heading for the Acheron. Judging by Tellus's expression, he still didn't like the situation. She understood his anger; she had dragged him into this.

"I'm going to ask you something that I don't want leaving this chamber," Raisa said. "Do either of you have any idea why people can't die, or why Nyx has abandoned us?"

"No," Pen lied, keeping her voice smooth despite her nerves.

"So you just maimed Vox to teach him a lesson, rather than kill him?" Raisa challenged. It nearly made Pen freeze.

She recovered quickly. "I hate those who prey on others. I'm not a hero by any means. I wanted him to suffer."

"And your odd question about the priest's body and head was just speculation?"

"We've heard stories," Tellus said. "Some that the body would get up to retrieve the head, others that blood and meat would shoot out of the neck and try to reconnect it. They were rumors, but we had hoped to learn more."

"Why?"

Tellus shrugged. "Curiosity mostly, but I agree with you that this is a problem."

"Is that why you are headed south? Everyone knows the Acheron is connected to Skiachora somehow."

"I had read something about the city of Taiphus experiencing something similar," Pen said. "About a month back I had my throat cut by a robber in the woods." She indicated the somewhat healed ring on her neck. Luckily, her hair was long enough to hide that fact it went around her neck.

"What happened?"

"All of my blood poured out like it should, but I didn't die. I lay there in the dirt for two days before I had the strength to move. It wasn't a miracle, so I wanted to find out why it happened. I went to the Stymphalian libraries and read that Taiphus had a similar occurrence. Captain Tellus chose to join me because a close friend of his is in pain from cancer."

Raisa turned to Tellus. "That true?"

"Aye," he said. "We met in that library and traded stories. My friend asked me to go with her to investigate as well. Staying by his side wasn't doing any good."

"I'm sorry about your friend," Raisa said sincerely.

"I'm sorry about Narciso," he echoed.

"If this curse is righted, he'll die."

"It might be best."

Raisa nodded and looked to the fire, taking a moment. "The Ragged Wolves are in danger because of this curse. We can't do our job if people can't die. Which means my family is threatened. I would like to let you go and find

Taiphus, hell, I'd even go with you, but the Wolves need me, and they can't see me falter in my decision or our rules."

It was clear that Tellus understood, because his eyes softened with empathy. He knew what it meant to stick to a difficult situation. Pen would have done anything for her family as well if she thought it was right.

"Once this merchant is taken care of," Pen said, using Raisa's own terms, "you'll let us go?"

"Yes," Raisa said. "How are you going to find the ruins of Taiphus anyway? They've been lost for centuries."

"The library provided some good leads," Tellus offered.

Raisa gave a quick nod. "Very well, let me show you where you can sleep. We leave on the morrow."

She led them through the archway into a winding corridor of rock. Niches carved into the walls at intervals held candles that provided light. Torches would have given off too much smoke and poison the air. The floor was level and worn from so many feet, but some rocks were still jagged.

Palrig and Daeson fell in behind them. Palrig still held the sack containing the priest's head.

They passed several smaller rooms furnished with cots and chests, some had chairs. One section opened into a kitchen area complete with dining table. How they got the table in there Pen had no idea; it looked like a single, solid piece of oak.

Raisa passed by it and took them to a small chamber similar to the others. There were only two cots and a barred gate as a door. Raisa ushered them inside, closing the gate and locking it. It was rusted in some spots but looked quite solid.

Pen hated the feeling of being locked away. The reassurance that at least she was conscious this time didn't help much. The thought of the little razor did, however.

"I'll send for a bucket of water and a cloth for you," Raisa said to Tellus. "You may be our prisoner, but I'm nothing if not civil."

"I'd appreciate that," Tellus replied.

Raisa left them, followed by Palrig. Daeson stayed behind, leaning on the opposite wall facing them, playing guard.

Rain fell that night, leaving the ground damp. Pen relished the clean air after spending a night in the cavern with the Ragged Wolves. Most of them were above ground now, mounting up their horses. Raisa had returned Phobos and Demos, thankfully, and sat atop her own black mare. Palrig and Daeson went with them along with three other Wolves. Pen wondered if they were some kind of escort to make sure they did their job.

"The walk isn't long," Raisa told Pen as they started along the southern edge of the river, heading west. "We'll be there long before nightfall."

"If you don't mind my asking, how did you get that scar?" Pen asked. She was curious, and she knew building a relationship with this woman might be useful later. People were always more willing to help friends than enemies.

"It's not as impressive as you might think," Raisa stated. "I fell down a well as a child, bashed my face on the side going down. I managed to tread water using the walls for support for six hours before anyone knew I was there."

Six hours down a well. Pen shuddered. It wasn't a grand fight story like she expected, but it still spoke of Raisa's resilience. Not to mention being scarred from youth probably prevented many suitors from pursuing her, possibly giving her father a hard time.

Yiga and Narciso had stayed behind, but the rest of them traveled quietly. One of them, a skinny archer named Braz, pulled ahead to act as a lookout. Soon the forest enveloped the narrow path.

Near midday Pen spotted a figure standing in the middle of the road. She turned to Tellus, but he'd already seen it too. His eyebrows knitted together in confusion: the figure looked wrong. He urged his horse on faster to reach Raisa, and Pen did the same.

Tellus was about to say something but Raisa stopped him. "I see it too."

As they drew closer Pen realized it was Braz. Another man stood behind him with a knife to his throat.

Raisa stopped, and the rest of the group followed suit.

"Drop your weapons and dismount," the man holding Braz ordered.

"Now why should I do that?" Raisa asked sweetly.

"I'll kill your man here."

"If he was caught by you, then he's not worth my time." Pen couldn't believe it, after all that talk of family, Raisa was willing to let Braz die.

Braz showed no sign of fear. Tension, yes, but he was calm. Perhaps Raisa's words were a ruse to confuse the man holding Braz hostage.

The forest around them came to life. More men and women revealed themselves. A couple aimed arrows.

"Drop your weapons," the man holding Braz demanded again.

Raisa stood her ground, appearing to weigh her options. Pen was ready to dismount, but she followed Raisa's lead. Tellus seemed to be analyzing the situation too.

"Above you!" Braz shouted.

The man cut his throat. Blood fountained down, coating his tunic. Braz fell, stunned and clutching at his neck as blood rushed over his hands.

At the same time, another man fell from the trees above them, landing on Raisa and her mare. He dragged her down, bashing her head on the ground.

All of the rotting Skiachora broke loose then. The archers fired. One arrow struck Daeson in the arm, the other hit Metis's horse. Daeson pulled the arrow from the meat of his arm. Metis's horse panicked and reared, throwing her off.

Demos panicked as the chaos broke out. Tellus drew his sword, still mounted, but Pen only had a knife. She gripped it now, jumping from Demos, hoping the animal wouldn't run off. Her father taught her how to fight in combat but never on a horse. She'd be useless on one.

A woman charged at Pen, screaming and brandishing a spear. Pen ducked under it, quickly dispatching the woman with the knife in her jaw. The woman dropped clutching the torn flesh.

Pen saw Tellus fighting two men; one had a club and struck Phobos's rump. Phobos stumbled, braying, nearly casting Tellus into the fray. Tellus recovered and lopped off the first man's arm, then turned to the other, parried his sword and stuck him in the gut.

Raisa had recovered and raised her battle axe. The man who had fallen on her now lay on the ground, unmoving, while she fought off two more bandits. One came at her with a sword, while the other, a woman, carried a small hammer and a shield. Raisa ducked under the first man's sword and swung at his arm. It didn't cut clean, but there was a satisfying crunch of bone, and the bandit dropped his sword. The woman with the hammer was more challenging. Raisa kicked at her shield, stunning her, and buried her axe in the woman's skull.

It was a mess of blades and bodies. Pen ducked under another bandit, stabbing him in his dominant arm as he swung at Metis. Pen got out of the way as Metis thrust at his throat.

A dog joined the fray, barking madly. Pen watched as it bounded out of the woods and made for Raisa. She must have attacked its master. Pen was too far away to help; she could only yell as the dog pounced at Raisa's back. Tellus rushed in, bleeding from several wounds but upright, and threw his arm up. The dog clamped down on his arm rather than Raisa's neck. Tellus screamed at the beast as the two of them fell wrestling to the ground. Raisa and Palrig struggled to pull the dog off him. Palrig gave the dog a swift kick, and it bounded off.

Raisa helped Tellus up. He now had no use of his left arm, but he continued to fight.

There were too many bandits. Braz was down, Tellus was wounded. Raisa seemed alright but her head was bleeding. Several of the bandits were on the ground, not dead but writhing or lying stunned, but most still stood.

In a few more moments the Wolves would be overrun.

Pen knelt by the edge of the road, holding her head to feign being injured. Using a cut on her forearm she didn't remember receiving, possibly from the woman with the spear, she drew out a tendril and snaked it into the forest.

The trees and foliage were thick, so she sent more. Keeping her blood thick, she struck one of the trees, then the one beside it. A couple of bandits and Wolves were distracted by the disturbance. She hit another tree farther down the road from her. There was too much blood outside her body, and she was getting dizzy.

Acting fast and keeping her blood low to the ground, she wrapped a tendril around one bandit's ankle and dragged him screaming into the woods. Once there she formed a spear and struck his throat, cutting off the scream. She grabbed another bandit in the same manner.

Everyone had stopped now, facing the woods. The trees shook with the strikes of what appeared to be a massive beast. Pen still crouched several yards away, but her vision was going dark.

Everyone was backing away. Pen grabbed one more bandit and threw her into the river, screaming. The rest of the bandits bolted.

She had used too much blood at once. It was harder to breathe, and black clouds covered her vision. She lost the connection, causing the blood to melt where it was, coating the trees and grass. She passed out.

Chapter Eleven

When she came to, the fire blinded her. Squeezing her eyes shut and moaning at the pain in her eyes, she rolled to her side.

"Take it easy."

A hand touched her arm, making her jump and grope for her knife, back in its makeshift sheath at her belt. She opened her eyes. It was Tellus who had touched her. He held up both hands in peace. She sighed and let go of her knife.

"Don't move too much." He helped her sit up and handed her a wineskin. The wine was sour but refreshing.

Pen spotted the bandage on his left arm. His sleeve had been cut away, and the white cloth had spots of red. He sat beside her and took a swig from the skin.

"What happened?" she asked.

"Not entirely sure, to be honest," he said. "During the fight something came out of the woods… tentacles, I suppose, and took some of the road bandits. The rest were scared off."

He fell silent, watching the others. Raisa was with Palrig and Metis, talking things over, while Daeson had wrapped a bandage around Braz's neck. His eyes were open, but

Pen wasn't sure he was conscious. The other, Lichas, kept watch.

"Was it you?" Tellus kept his voice quiet, the wineskin at his lips.

"Yes," Pen answered in a whisper.

Tellus nodded and took another swig. Pen held out her hand. He gave her the skin, and she swallowed too.

She realized the shadows were different; they were too long. "How long has it been?"

"Couple of hours. They couldn't move Braz, and given your injury, it was best to let you lie still. I told them I saw one of them hit you over the head with a rock. That's why you passed out."

"Thank you." She was surprised he had kept her secret hidden, but given his policy to lay low, it made sense.

He just nodded.

Raisa left Palrig and Metis to join them.

"How are you feeling?" she asked Pen, still standing.

"I'm alright," Pen said.

"Are you sure? Head injuries can be misleading."

Pen took stock of her symptoms. "Dizzy, mostly, bit of a headache."

"Alright. We'll have to keep an eye on you, because we're moving out."

"Now? What about Braz?" Tellus asked.

"Daeson is taking him back." She turned to Pen again. "You survived a cut like that before?"

At first Pen had no idea what Raisa was talking about, she touched her own neck, feeling the remanence of the scab from the guillotine blade. Then she remembered the lie about having her throat cut on the road instead, "Yes, it took a few days to even move, but yes."

"Good. Daeson will probably have to carry him on his own horse. A couple of the other horses ran off, and your brown one can't walk."

"Phobos?"

"If that's what you call him. He can limp but he can't carry anyone."

Pen stood and wobbled. Tellus went to help, but she waved him off. Once she was up, she was relatively fine.

"So how many horses do we have?" Tellus asked.

"Five."

"Not so bad. At least only one of us has to walk."

Raisa grimaced. "I suppose."

Pen noticed the pile of bodies at the side of the road. The bandits had been dispatched and left on top of each other.

"Where are the heads?" Pen asked, slightly nauseous.

Raisa followed her gaze. "Oh, we kept them. Daeson is taking them back too. They'll be put with the priest."

"Is that necessary?" Tellus asked.

"I don't bloody care at this point. They attacked us." Despite her defence, she didn't seem happy.

She left before either of them could reply. "Lichas! Come back, we're leaving."

Lichas helped Daeson tie Braz to his gray warhorse. Daeson mounted and galloped back the way they had come.

Tellus took the saddle off Phobos. While he moved the bags to Demos's saddle, Pen went to comfort Phobos. He was calm but twitchy and couldn't put pressure on his back leg.

Raisa came up behind her. "We can't put him down, and Daeson couldn't take the time to get him to our cavern. But he can go free. With a bit of luck his leg will heal and he'll be fine."

Or he could get eaten by wolves without dying. Pen kept that thought to herself. There was nothing she could do for him.

"Raisa!" Lichas trotted up to them. "I was doing one last sweep to make sure we got them all. I found a huge amount of blood coating the trees where that thing had been."

Pen's heart nearly stopped. Tellus had heard as well and joined them.

"Maybe the bandits killed something there?" Raisa suggested.

"I thought so too," Lichas said, "but there's too much, spanning at least a dozen feet across. It's only in that one area as well. There's no evidence that whatever it was had been dragged away or moved itself. There's a thin line of blood leading to the road but then nothing."

Raisa frowned. "It could have been what attacked the bandits."

"Maybe, given that its arms were red too, but where did it go? And why not kill us too?" Lichas was clearly disturbed by his discovery.

"I don't know, and I don't want to. Now get on your horse and let's move," Raisa commanded. "The quicker we're out of here the better."

They mounted the remaining horses. Raisa still had her black mare. Palrig, under orders from Raisa, dismounted his horse to allow Tellus to ride it.

The path wound through the woods but the river remained in sight. At every bend in the road Pen's heart quickened with anticipation of another attack, but they were left alone for the rest of the journey.

When night fell, they could see lanterns marking the village. Raisa let them rest for a couple of hours while she came up with a plan: she wanted to make sure the entire village was asleep before they moved in.

It was a simple fishing village with buildings constructed of wood and mud brick. From what Pen could make out in the moonlight, there was a large storehouse by the docks. There was also a house on a hill, slightly larger than the others. That must be the estate of either the rich merchant or the mayor of the village.

They all sat around the fire, dining on roasted deer that Palrig had caught. He was a brute to be sure, he had fought off the bandits with his claymore and then, when he had dropped it, a large branch, but he seemed to enjoy cooking. While rotating the deer carcass over their fire, he rubbed salt and herbs into the meat, watching it sizzle.

A thought struck Pen: the deer was dead. She scolded herself for not noticing it before. Whatever the nature of the curse, it was only affecting humans.

"We move in when the moon rises tomorrow night," Raisa said between mouthfuls of deer.

"I thought we were doing this tonight," Tellus protested. He probably wanted to get it over with. Pen didn't blame him.

"I wanted to, but given the surprise on the road, we're going to take tonight and tomorrow to rest. Lichas and Metis, you two will follow the directions his partner gave us and find the merchant's house. Once your back the rest of us will enter the house and make sure Tellus does his part to kill the merchant."

Tellus turned sullen. Pen knew he didn't want to do this, but the wait was probably killing him. She didn't know if he'd be able to take the merchant's head.

The following night came all too soon. Lichas and Metis had returned before sunset, having found the merchant's home by the storehouse. Since Lichas was the best tracker, and they had already found the house, he stayed behind to watch the camp. When the crescent moon was high, Raisa, Palrig, and Metis, accompanied by Pen and Tellus, entered the village.

Metis led them to the back door of a two storey building made of wood beside the storehouse. The house itself was simple, and it looked almost new. Everything was quiet, except for the occasional bark of a dog. When they approached the door, Metis knelt, taking a pair of small lock picks from her pocket. Raisa and Palrig turned their backs to watch the road; unfortunately, there was no natural cover. Pen could tell they were well practiced at this.

Tellus looked sick.

Pen spotted two figures walking along the road toward them. Palrig shielded Metis with his body while she worked. Pen did her best to look casual, crossing her arms and leaning against the wall.

There was a soft click, and Metis stood as she opened the door. They were about to sneak inside when the figures on the road spotted them. They paused, probably afraid. One touched the other's arm and they turned away. They weren't running in a panic, but they weren't calm.

"Fuck. Palrig, Metis, after them. Meet back at the camp in one hour," Raisa directed. "I'll get this done."

Palrig and Metis took off into the shadows.

Raisa held the door open just enough for Pen and Tellus to enter. Tellus didn't move at first. Pen shoved him forward. She was slight, but it was enough to get him moving.

They entered the house through the kitchens. Bread loaves rested on the counters, along with a basket of apples, and the stove looked freshly cleaned.

"You two up front," Raisa whispered. "Look for a staircase. The bedrooms are probably on the second floor."

"Why have us go first?" Tellus hissed. "You're the trained assassin."

"I need to make sure you do your job," she snapped. "Now move."

They did. The kitchen led to the dining room and a hallway. The craftsmanship of the building and furniture were simple, from what Pen could tell in the moonlight, but well taken care of.

They found the staircase leading up, and Pen went first. Stepping lightly, she was able to find the parts of the wood that made the least amount of noise. Tellus and Raisa followed her steps. The second floor began with another hallway that ended ending on the right but led around a corner on the left.

They checked the doors; all were open except one. Pen found a locked door.

"This might be the main bedchamber," she whispered to Raisa in the gloom.

"Maybe," Raisa said, "but I want to check the others around the corner first. Keep this one in mind."

Tellus opened another door and froze. Pen couldn't see his face in the gloom, so she came closer and looked into the room. She could see his strained horror now. He had opened a child's bedroom where there was a little girl asleep.

Pen's heart went out to the girl. Her life was about to be ruined, or at least drastically altered in the absence of her father.

"I can't do this," Tellus breathed.

Raisa was further down the hall, checking another door, and hadn't heard.

With numb fingers, Pen took the door handle from Tellus. She closed the door on the sleeping girl.

"You have to, or she'll take your head."

Tellus just looked at her, then at Raisa, with a mix of dread and hatred.

Raisa glanced up and gestured to them to follow her. Pen waited until Tellus moved.

The last door at the end of the hall was also unlocked. Pen made a mental note that if she ever got her own home again, she'd have locks on every door, especially the bedchambers. Raisa stuck her head inside, then gestured to them to enter ahead of her. Pen practically had to drag Tellus inside.

It was the bedchamber. There was a desk littered with papers and a large bed with a single man sleeping in it.

"Fuck," Raisa said.

She was looking at something along the hall, in the direction from which they had come. Pen peeked around the door frame. A woman with a candle was walking toward them. Her head was down and she rubbed her eyes.

Raisa poked Tellus on the shoulder to get his attention. She then jabbed her finger at the man asleep. The expression in her eyes was hard as steel. She bounded into the hall after the woman, probably the man's wife. Pen heard a quick scuffle, a squeak of a stifled scream, then the candle went out.

Pen and Tellus were alone. Pen approached the sleeping man, the rug muffling the sound of her steps. She couldn't judge the color of his hair in the dark, but it was light. His beard was the same. He slept on his stomach, bare chested, oblivious to the dangers around him.

Pen turned to Tellus. He hadn't moved. He looked like he was going to vomit.

"Tellus, you have to do this," Pen stated. She didn't like it any more than he did, but she forced herself to think of it as another obstacle between her and her family.

"I can't do this." His voice was dead.

"You have to."

"I won't. I won't murder an innocent man."

"You don't know if he's innocent."

"You don't know if he's guilty!" he whispered.

"Raisa will take both our heads if you don't!"

Tellus was about to protest again, but a creak in the floorboards, so loud in the silence that it might have been cannon fire, made him pause. There was nothing after that. Pen imagined Raisa coming closer along the hall.

Pen stepped forward, grabbed the hilt of Tellus's sword, and unsheathed it before he could protest. Using the momentum, she managed to angle the blade at the sleeping man's neck. It didn't cut clean through, but Pen felt as well as heard his spine crunch. The man was awake now, eyes bulging, but unable to scream. Pen swung the heavy blade once more and severed the head. Blood sprayed over the headboard and soaked the sheets.

Pen tossed the head to Tellus, who caught it. He looked as stunned and pained as the merchant. She pressed the bloody sword into his hand as Raisa appeared in the doorway.

She took one look at Tellus then the head in his hands and nodded.

"Good, let's get out of here."

The wife was sitting slumped against the wall.

"Ah." Tellus might have wanted to say more but didn't.

"Relax," Raisa said, "she's just unconscious."

They met Lichas back at the campfire. He reported to Raisa that his time was uneventful. He sounded bored and disappointed that he couldn't "join in on the fun," as he put it.

Pen couldn't stop thinking of the merchant's eyes as she had crushed his spine. She sat and stared at the fire, hoping to burn away the image.

Tellus sat against a tree, away from the firelight and the main group. He began cleaning his blade but kept wiping it even when the blood was gone. His eyes were as cold as the steel blade.

Palrig and Metis returned with two more heads. One was a woman's. Bile rose in Pen's throat when she saw them. Metis told Raisa these two had seen them breaking in, as Raisa had thought. The sack they had brought with them was large enough to hold all three heads. Raisa tied the sack to her mare for the journey home. She suggested they get a few hours of sleep, then leave before dawn.

"What about the woman in the house?" Pen asked. "Won't she wake up?"

"The potion on the cloth I held to her nose and mouth is strong enough to keep her asleep for at least eight hours," Raisa explained.

Metis volunteered to keep watch in order to give Lichas a rest, and they settled around the fire to sleep. The Ragged Wolves settled. Pen lay down but kept watching the flames dance. She wondered what a person would feel if they were burned alive but couldn't die. Even if they were incinerated to a skeletal husk, what would happen?

Tellus sat alone by his tree. His sword was in his lap, polished clean, while his head rested against the trunk. Pen didn't think he'd be able to sleep much tonight either.

She couldn't stop thinking of those heads. Did they still feel the pain from their bodies? Did their bodies decay? How would the rope of the noose feel as it dug into a person's throat, cutting off all air? Or if someone were drawn and quartered? Or trampled by horses? Or drowning, what would water filling the lungs be like?

A couple of hours passed, and then Pen stood. Metis had kept the fire burning and watched her as she got up.

"Just have to make water." Pen said casually.

She walked deep into the forest where no one would hear her. She doubled over and retched. She could still see the man's eyes.

Footsteps behind her immediately made her go for the knife. It was Tellus. He looked as tired as she felt. She was about to ask what he was doing here when she vomited again. Tellus came closer and put a hand on her shoulder.

Chapter Twelve

Pen had to set her cup down from laughing so much. Metis had just finished telling the story of how she caught a deer from a tree but fell out shortly after and landed on another one. She'd been able to ride it like a horse for some time before jumping off.

Tellus sat with them in the kitchens. He was grinning. His arm was still bandaged but was healing properly now. When they returned to the Ragged Wolves' cavern, infection had set in, causing the bite to swell. They opted to stay for a couple of days, at Raisa's offer, to let it heal. He was lucky it hadn't worsened or spread.

Raisa sat at the head of the oak dining table, an empty plate before her, like the rest of them. Pen couldn't help but admire Raisa for everything she worked for. The Ragged Wolves might be assassins, but they had standards and were well led.

"You have to stop picking at it," Raisa said to Tellus. She said it jokingly, but there was real concern.

Pen glanced over in time to see Tellus arrange his sleeve back over the bandage. "I'm aware, but the itch is maddening."

The laughter died on Pen's lips. She understood all too well what a maddening itch felt like.

Raisa chuckled. "I never did ask why you didn't take that opportunity with the bandits to run?"

"I've been thinking of that too, actually. I'm a bit of an idiot for not taking the chance, but I didn't want to lose my foot or head. Besides, Pen was unconscious, and with this bite there was no way I could have carried her. You would have caught us quickly."

"Aye, we would have." Raisa smirked. "I was wondering when you planned to go actually, now that your end of the bargain is done."

Part of Pen didn't want to go. There was a bed here, and the people were kind to her. There was also an abundance of food she didn't have to fight for or steal. But all of that was overshadowed by the anticipation of coming closer to her own family.

"I think the morning would be a good time to go?" Tellus looked at Pen, directing the question at her.

"Dawn will be fine," she agreed.

"You two are welcome to stay, even join us if you want. As long as you clean up after yourself, I don't see any problem."

Tellus didn't say anything. Perhaps he wasn't sure how to decline without sounding rude.

"We appreciate the offer, Raisa, but Taiphus awaits," Pen said.

"Of course, that should be exciting," Raisa said. "You'll have to come back and tell us about it when you find it."

Lichas was about to share a story that he said rivaled Metis's when a young woman, perhaps in her mid-twenties, entered. She looked worried. She approached

Raisa timidly, handed her a scrap of parchment, then scurried away.

Pen watched as Raisa's expression turned sour as she read the note. The sour look turned to pure hatred. Raisa stood and stormed off, almost knocking over her goblet.

Pen and Tellus exchanged glances. He seemed just as surprised as she was.

A couple of hours later they were in the room allocated to them by Raisa. There was a limited number of bedchambers, so they had to share, but at least this room didn't have a locked gate. It didn't have a door at all, which meant no privacy, but they were free to roam.

Some hours later, Raisa knocked on the stone to get their attention. Tellus had been checking his pack again, while Pen passed the time with a game of Solace with some cards Metis had sold her.

"Tellus," Raisa said. She sounded distressed, almost cautionary. "Queen Aethra is going to be attacked."

The belted dagger strapped to the boot Tellus held clattered to the floor. Pen looked up from her cards, too shocked to respond. Why the queen of Stymphalia? What good would that do?

"What?" Tellus looked like he'd been punched.

"I thought I should let you know, given you're captain of the Guard there," Raisa stated quietly.

"How do you know this?"

"The courier at dinner gave me a message written by my spy in Kalymnos. The king there has sent a rogue assassin to kill her. I don't know why. Probably some political strategy to weaken Stymphalia."

Tellus snatched up the dagger and belted his sword.

"What are you doing?" Pen asked, practically dreading the answer.

"Going back."

Pen felt stunned that he would abandon his journey and an order from his dying friend.

"I know this is bad," she said, standing, "but there's nothing you can do from here, and you probably won't get there in time. Raisa, how old is the message?"

"Five days, a week at most."

Tellus threw on his cloak. "Doesn't matter."

"What about A-our journey to Taiphus!" She'd nearly said the Acheron.

Tellus grabbed his pack and pushed past Raisa, who looked equally surprised.

Pen chased after him and blocked his path. "You're going to disobey a direct order from your king?" She kept her voice quiet, hoping Raisa didn't hear as she caught up.

"Protecting Aethra and the royal family is more important right now."

"He can't hurt her right now anyway. He can't physically kill her," she argued.

"And the alternative of him keeping her head is better?! Who knows what that will do to the baby?"

"He might not know that trick yet. He'll probably just cut her throat and run off." That did not sound like a good alternative, but she was rushed.

"You don't know that. I am not letting any harm come to her." Tellus pushed past her, heading to the Ragged Wolves' makeshift stables, a large cave with a hidden opening into a grove of trees.

"I'll go," Raisa called after him.

Tellus stopped and half turned back. "You'll go and defend the queen? Why?"

"Because you and Pen did us a service, twice," Raisa replied. "Granted, I forced the second one, but you still carried it out. And you didn't run when you had the chance. I even trust you enough to let you join us, and that is no trifling thing. Besides, I think I know who the king of Kalymnos is sending. A… friend of mine used to talk about that king like an old friend with peculiar tastes. I know how that man works."

Tellus hesitated, clearly debating whether he ought to protect the queen himself or send a friend. The friend, being a skilled assassin with connections, might be difficult for him to reconcile, but she'd get the job done. Pen could tell he was also torn between following his king or protecting his queen.

Tellus ran a hand through his hair. "You will let me know the outcome either way?"

"I will," Raisa promised. "Once it's done I will have word sent here waiting for you. Along with messages sent to my spies in neighboring city-states, should you pass through them."

Tellus sighed, not liking letting another do his work. "Fine. Will you leave tonight?"

"I'll leave at dawn. You know galloping through the countryside in the dark is suicide. Besides, the gates of Potamus are closed for the night anyway. You wouldn't have been able to get through any more than I could."

"I doubt that."

Raisa shrugged. "Well, we do have our ways, but daylight is safer."

"Very well," Tellus said reluctantly. He sounded tired.

Pen could breathe again. She led Tellus back to their chamber. Raisa left them to prepare for her own journey.

Tellus threw the pack in the corner and sat on his cot, holding his head. Pen sat on her cot facing him, unsure how to comfort him.

"I'm glad you didn't go," she admitted. She wasn't sure herself why she was glad, and Tellus didn't ask.

"Raisa will keep Queen Aethra safe," she said. "We may even get news of Aegeus."

Tellus stared at the floor, silent.

"Why are you so eager to go back now and delay your last promise to your friend?"

"Because Aethra was always kind to me." He still gazed at the floor, but it was as if he were seeing his queen. "And she saved my life once."

"You love her." Pen saw it in his eyes.

Tellus didn't reply.

"You're in love with your best friend's wife," Pen said, more surprised than anything. "Not only that, but she's the queen."

"I have never let these feelings get in the way of my job or theirs," Tellus said sharply. "Neither of them even know of this. I would not put Aegeus in that situation, or Aethra. They are happy together, which is rare for an arranged royal marriage, and I will not get in the middle of it. The bards alone would have the news spread like wildfire."

Pen stayed quiet. He'd been holding that in for a long while, probably his entire career.

"You won't tell anyone, will you?" There was the first hint of fear Pen had ever seen in his eyes.

"No, I'll take this to my grave."

Tellus took a breath. He was shaking slightly. "I've never said it out loud before."

"Technically, you didn't. I did."

Tellus scoffed. He took off his sword and lay in his cot still wearing his cloak. He turned away from Pen.

Pen blew out the lantern and lay down to sleep, hoping dawn would come quickly.

Chapter Thirteen

After a week of straight horseback riding through more hills and small mountains, Pen and Tellus reached the forest north of the Acheron. Maps and the accounts of travelers suggested the river was just on the other side of the trees. What maps failed to share, but travelers often complained of, was that it took nearly another whole day to cross the forest. Most travelers said it was too dangerous and should be avoided entirely. Others even said it was haunted, and people had gone missing. Tellus said that was ridiculous, but no one would believe them if they said people couldn't die.

They camped at the edge of the trees as night fell. Riding into a forest in the dark would be dangerous for the horses, one of which they had bought from the Ragged Wolves that Pen had names Zay, and they could easily get lost. The trees were dense, and there was no clear path. The road on which they had been traveling veered east alongside the woods.

Pen sat on a fallen trunk and produced her cards. "Care for a game?"

Tellus looked up from the dagger he'd been sharpening. "Thank you, but no."

Pen shrugged, not minding that he didn't want to play. She had been used to traveling on her own for so long; her offer had been only a courtesy. She wouldn't have minded playing a round or two with him, though, since she enjoyed his company.

The scraping of whetstone on steel stopped. Pen looked up and caught Tellus looking north again.

"You're still worried about Aethra?" She knew the answer. He would look behind them almost every hour as if expecting a messenger to run up to them.

Concern lined his face. "Yes. We haven't stopped in any other city, so Raisa's people can't reach us."

Pen was about to suggest taking a detour to the nearest village, Zenyu, and see if they could catch any news. That would mean days of backtracking, though.

"We could go to the town close by," Tellus murmured, "but that would take too long."

It was like he had read her mind. She laughed. Tellus turned to face her, confused.

"I had thought the same thing," she admitted.

That tugged a half smile out of him. It was the most she had seen all week.

"So." She let the word hang for a moment, and when she knew she still had Tellus's attention she asked, "How did you and Aethra meet?"

He looked crestfallen, but Pen caught the spark in his eye at the mention of her name. "That's not something I should encourage."

"Oh come on, it's a bit late for that, don't you think?" He already loved her, there was no denying it.

Tellus didn't reply for a long time, and when she thought he never would, he spoke. "It was during the day the betrothal was announced. She and her father came to Stymphalia from Kalymnos so their fathers could make a peace treaty."

"Wait, she's from Kalymnos?'

"Aye."

"Then why is her father trying to have her killed?"

"Her father passed away ten years ago. Her cousin sits on the throne there now," he explained.

"But he's still family?" she asked, dumbfounded.

"My guess is that her child will have equal rights to both Stymphalia and Kalymnos, thus causing him problems in the future should he refuse to step down."

"So he's not actually their king, just a figurehead?"

"Yes, until Aethra's child, should it be a son, comes of age."

"That's why their fathers had them marry," Pen said with dawning realization. She had never followed politics or royal family trees, but it made sense.

"Exactly. Now, it wasn't like the stories. I didn't fall head over heels at the first sight of her, though she was beautiful. I was a trainee guard at the time, seventeen I think, so I was staying in the corner, watching the crowd at the feast. The more experienced stayed closer to the royalty at their head table. I saw a man walk up behind her and fill her goblet with wine. He then took out a small blade, unafraid of the crowd or guards. She must have seen a glint of metal or saw a reflection in the crystal of her goblet, because before I could shout the princess sprang to her feet, completely bewildering Aegeus, and smashed the goblet in the assassin's face. The guards tackled him then and carried him off. That was when I realized she was not only beautiful but strong and fearless. The… deeper feelings started to grow after that. I never spoke of it to Aegeus because he was seeing the same thing I saw in her. It wasn't my place, as a lowly orphan from the kitchens turned city guard, to come between my best friend and his betrothed, let alone two kingdoms.

"As I moved up the ranks, they were both happy for me. Aethra would sometimes confide her worries to me when Aegeus went hunting. Aegeus would charge me with staying by her side whenever he had to leave the city, especially when she began to grow with child. Aegeus and I have always been close as brothers, and Aethra even said she saw me as a brother-in-law."

Tellus fell silent. No man wanted to be seen as a brother by the woman he loved. Pen wanted to ask him how he'd become an orphan, if he knew his parents, but she let that rest.

He forced a breath.

"So," he said, either mimicking her or distracting himself, "tell be about your family. The ones you lost?"

"What?" Her heart nearly seized.

"You asked me about my loved ones, now tell me about yours."

"I… um," she stammered. She didn't want to open that buried box.

Tellus looked concerned at her distress. She hated herself for not hiding it better.

"How long have you been alone, Pen?" he asked gently.

She swallowed, trying to force down the sudden lump in her throat. "Since they died."

"When was that?"

"Three months ago." She didn't want to talk about this, but she'd made Tellus talk, so it was only fair.

"That's close to when this curse started," he speculated. "They might have been the last few."

Pen couldn't say more. She didn't want to think back to that time. Their deaths, she had buried them under the willow tree, but after that her mind was black. Black as her heart and grief. She closed her eyes, mimicking that blackness, wanting to drown in it.

She hadn't seen him get up, but her eyes opened again as she felt him sit next to her. He took the deck of cards from her clenched hands. They were almost bent in half.

"You need to talk about this, Pen," he said softly. "Letting it fester will do you no good. I can vouch for that personally. Since I've admitted my love for Aethra out loud, I've felt lighter for it, even though nothing will come of it."

He continued when she refused to speak. "You had said you killed them. That it was an accident?"

It felt like a knife had wrenched her heart.

"Yes," she whispered.

"How?"

It all came flooding out like a dam had broken. She told him of her wrists, how her power had awakened, and how it killed Arch and Alard. She was left shaking. Tears streaked down her cheeks as she stared at the fire.

She jumped when Tellus touched her shoulder. He left his hand there. She had forgotten what a kind human touch was like.

"That's why you're going to the Acheron, to save them?"

She could only nod.

At dawn they covered the fire and gathered Demos and Zay's reins. The trees were too dense and the branches were too low to ride them. The horses avoided the branches, but the ground was uneven with rocks and roots. The roots were so thick and exposed that they looked like knobby hands gripping the earth. The forest consisted mostly of oak and maple trees, with the occasional pine. The sky was hardly visible through the canopy, and the light that did make it through was cast green.

They didn't talk much about the previous night, nor did Pen want to. Their conversations consisted mostly of "careful, there's a hole here" and "we'll have to go around the log."

Around midday, Pen began watching the trees around them for anything to eat. There wasn't much except the occasional squirrel or rabbit; even birds seemed scarce.

A figure cut across her line of sight between two trees. It was quick but human. It was trying to hide behind a maple tree. Pen could see the small figure shifting.

"Tellus, hold on!" she called.

He was only a few yards ahead with Zay.

"What is it?" he called back.

"I saw something," she replied, quickly tying Demos to a branch.

Pen made her way to the figure. It didn't run away. Moving closer, she saw that it was a little girl. She was crouched by the tree trunk in a crudely made leather dress. Her brown hair stuck out at odd angles. She watched Pen, unafraid. She couldn't have been more than five or six.

Pen knelt down next to her. "Hello."

Tellus caught up with her and saw the girl. She looked up at him; she didn't run but did now appear scared.

"No wait, it's okay," Pen said gently. "This is my friend."

She calmed a bit, but her eyes darted between them.

"What's your name?" Pen asked.

"Samae," she replied.

"My name is Pen, and this is Tellus. Are you lost?"

"No."

"You're not?" Tellus asked, confused. "Where do you live?"

Samae stood up, more confident, pointing west into the trees. "That way."

Pen stood too. "Why don't we take you back. Don't want your parents getting worried."

"Okay. Papa will be happy too. He says people don't come and visit anymore." She was quite at ease now, probably assuming these strangers could be her friends.

"It shouldn't take too long, if you just wondered off a bit," Tellus said. "Let's get you home."

Samae grabbed Pen's hand and followed them to their horses. She giggled when Pen lifted her onto Demos's saddle.

"Careful of the branches," Pen cautioned.

Tellus gathered Zay's reins and they diverted in the direction Samae indicated.

"So where are you from?" Tellus asked Samae.

"Just a village. Papa said it doesn't have a name."

That was odd; every village or town had a name. Come to think of it, Pen couldn't think of any settlements in these woods except the extinct Taiphus.

Samae really hadn't wandered far; they only had to walk for about ten minutes or so when the trees ended and they found themselves in a clearing. There were only five small cabins made of the local wood, situated around a central fire pit with tall torches in a circle.

Around two dozen people milled about. They were dressed in a similar fashion as Samae and had similar complexions, with blue or brown hair. They must be a single family.

Samae squirmed, and Tellus set her on the ground. She ran over to a short woman with dark blue hair and hugged her. Then she exclaimed, "I brought friends."

The woman, presumably her mother, asked, "Where did you find her?"

"She was playing in the trees," Tellus explained. "We thought she was lost."

A man jogged over. His hair was the same shade as the girl's. She let go of her mother and hugged his leg.

"Are you alright, little flower?" he asked, kneeling to her level.

"Yes, Papa. And I brought friends."

He stood turning to Pen and Tellus, beaming. "Thank you. My daughter can be a little adventurous. I'm sorry she bothered you."

"It was no bother," Pen said. "I just wanted to make sure she was safe."

"Many people would have done worse if they came across a lost girl. Let us thank you properly. We will prepare a feast."

"There's no need, but thank you," Tellus said politely. "We must be on our way."

The man's jubilance faded. "Please stay. We don't get many visitors, and I can't possibly let you leave without some gesture of gratitude."

Before Tellus could refuse, Pen said, "Staying one night should be fine, but we'll leave at dawn."

"Of course." He practically bowed to her. "You must be traveling somewhere important if you're in this forest."

Tellus grimaced at her but didn't argue. He probably wanted rest as much as she did.

The man turned to the gathered crowd. "Tonight we feast!"

They cheered; Samae was laughing too. Pen couldn't help but join in their happiness. Samae came over, took Pen's hand, and led her away. Looking back, Pen saw Tellus engulfed by a crowd asking questions. They really must not get visitors often.

As night fell, the great fire pit was lit, along with the ring of torches. A couple of the townsfolk brought out drums and began playing a deep tribal beat. The father of Samae, named Camus, gave Pen a small cup of a thick, sour liquid. Once she got past the oddly bitter taste, it was rather pleasant. The world seemed a little brighter. Tellus received the same brew and asked Camus the name of their village.

Camus laughed and explained good naturedly that the village was so small they didn't bother with a name. It wasn't so much a town as a single family anyway.

Pen sat in the grass with Samae and their odd ale in hand, laughing too loudly at the slightest thing. She was fascinated by the fire, as well; it was like she could see the light itself dancing around her with the people. She stood and started dancing with everyone. They spun and swirled around the fire like the light. She wanted to stay here forever; she saw Tellus was having an equally good time with a local girl with dark blue hair on his arm.

She spun and danced with the music and light. Then the ground rushed up to meet her and the light was gone.

When Pen woke up it was still dark. Groaning from the splitting headache, she went to stand but smacked her head on a piece of wood. That pain woke her completely, and she realized she was in a small cage. Why in the bloody name of Nyx was she always passing out and waking up imprisoned?

Tellus was in another cage beside her. He was able to get on his knees. The cages were made to be comfortable for a dog, not a human. He looked just as confused as she felt.

The light of the fire still reached them, though it didn't dance anymore. Pen saw Demos spinning slowly, roasting on a spit over the fire. They had cut his throat and taken his legs off. Zay was in the process of being gutted by a laughing man with light hair and a scar on his left arm. The fire might not be dancing for Pen anymore, but the villagers were still spinning around it.

"Those bastards!" Pen shouted.

The man, Camus, heard her and strode over. He knelt before the cages.

"Your daughter wasn't lost, was she?" Tellus demanded.

"Actually, she was. I had no idea she'd bring two extra morsels with her." Camus smiled.

"We save your daughter and you eat our horses? Then lock us in cages?" Pen wanted to gouge his eyes out. She went for her knife, but it was gone. Tellus didn't have his weapons either.

"I said *we* were going to feast," Camus shrugged, "and you two are the most important guests of honor who get to be sacrificed to Nyx. Although with the amount of horse flesh you've provided, you might have to wait until tomorrow night. I hope you don't mind."

He stood and left them, heading back to the gathering.

"What does *that* mean?" Pen said, frustrated and sitting back in her cage.

"I've heard of tribes like this," Tellus said. "This is probably why people are going missing."

"Wait, they're *eating* people?" Eating the horses was barbaric enough.

"We have to get out," Tellus said. He pulled at the lock, but it wouldn't budge, even though it was quite corroded.

Pen's lock was just as solid. Panic rushed through her veins, but she refused to be afraid. She turned that panic into determination to survive. It had saved her before.

Tellus was stretching his arm through his cage for a rock, but it was out of reach, no matter how much he stretched. He cursed, pulling his arm back.

Pen dug into her sleeve for her hidden pocket. Her razor was still there, thank the gods. She had wanted to keep this little weapon a secret, but in the face of cannibalism she didn't care. She took the razor in hand. It went deeper than she intended, but her hand had twitched with the adrenaline.

Tellus had seen, but she didn't care. The rabble was too drunk on ale, dancing and gorging on Demos, to pay any attention to them. Pen drew her blood to the rusty lock and opened it. Moving as carefully as she could while practically crawling, she opened the cage and climbed out. It was well constructed, with solid iron hinges. Tellus's cage was the same, but the lock opened just as easily.

"Have you had that razor the entire time?" he asked quietly.

"Yes." The razor was tucked safely into her sleeve again as she helped Tellus out of his cage. He was significantly bigger than her, and the opening was built for a dog.

They crept to the tree line. The fire light didn't reach them here, but their empty cages were exposed. Pen would have liked to put some kind of dummy in them, but it was impossible. They ducked behind the trees into the shadows.

"My sword," Tellus cursed. He turned back, looking for the weapons.

"Just leave it, we can find another." Pen wanted nothing more than to run, even though a part of her wanted to eradicate these cannibals.

"Aegeus gave me that sword," he protested.

Before she could respond, he left the safety of the trees. Keeping low to the ground, he snuck behind one of the cabins. That was when Pen saw their weapons on the porch of that cabin in plain sight of the crowd. Now who was being reckless?

She cursed and clung to her tree, watching as Tellus kept his back to the wall and slid toward the porch. He was in full view of the crowd, but they hadn't noticed him. Pen's nails dug into the bark.

When he got close enough, he made a grab for the weapons hanging on the railing. The belt of his sword was caught on a rail. Tellus kept his calm and worked the belt free. Weapons in hand, Tellus made it back behind the cabin and trotted to Pen. She could finally breathe again.

A young man by the fire tripped as he spun and fell laughing. He sprang up, facing them. His laughter died when he spotted Tellus. He shouted, pointing to them.

Tellus chanced one look behind and took off in a sprint, waving at Pen.

She didn't need any encouragement. She launched off the tree and took off into the forest, hoping Tellus was close behind. The now furious rabble was close; she could hear them shouting.

She couldn't watch where she was going because the branches clawed at her eyes, but she couldn't look to her feet because of the uneven ground. She remembered the fall while trying to escape Stymphalia. She ran on the balls of her feet, launching herself off roots and rocks.

She glimpsed Tellus to her left. His longer legs took him farther. He didn't pass Pen, though. She hoped he wasn't tiring.

An arrow thunked into a tree, close to her ear. Another disappeared in the foliage above her. She veered right, risking a glance back. It looked like the entire damned village was after them, and almost all of them had bows. Pen kept running.

They were too close, and there were too many of them. Pen formed a sword and solidified her blood. She shouted to Tellus, trying to give some indication of her place before ducking behind a boulder. There was no way of knowing if he'd seen.

The young man who had spotted them was searching beside the boulder. He had a bow but nothing else. Keeping low, Pen cut the tendon behind his ankle. Blood spurted over his sandal, and he crumpled, screaming. His friend caught up to him.

Pen ran around the boulder, coming up behind them and forming another sword. She took out two by stabbing their throats. More were behind them. Men and women carrying bows and axes; a couple only had hoes.

Pen used the trees to avoid their attacks, hacking at limbs and tendons, trying to keep her feet. Her blood boiled, not with panic but with battle rage. She removed hands from wrists, cut throats and tendons as she fought. She was skilled; her father had taught her well, but these people knew the woods better than she did. They appeared before her again and again, as if birthed from the trees themselves.

Once an opening presented itself, Pen took off again. She had no idea how she had avoided being wounded; blades had been flying everywhere. She couldn't tell how many she attacked as she ran among the trees.

She emerged into the clearing with the five cabins.

"Fuck!"

That curse cost her; every head turned to her. Most of them had gone into the forest, but not all. The remaining villagers rushed her with hoes and pitchforks. They had reach, but Pen relied on her speed and instincts.

A man stabbed with a pitchfork; she sidestepped and opened his stomach, spilling intestines. She followed through, cutting off the arm of a woman and stabbing another in the neck.

There were still five more: three woman and two men. Pen gained distance between them and ran around the fire pit. Demos was still skewered there, one side of him burning.

They tried to surround her by the fire, but Pen knocked over a couple of torches. One struck a woman, who screamed as flames engulfed her. The other torch knocked into a cabin, and sparks flew everywhere. Some caught on the thatch roof. The destruction of the home was enough of a distraction for Pen to enter the woods again. The firelight caught up to her now. She didn't need to look back to know the fire was spreading; the roar was enough.

The trees weren't so dense any more. The fire was moving quicker than she thought. In her haste, Pen ran into a branch. As she toppled over a hand darted out and grabbed her arm, straightening her. Trees didn't have hands, nor did they yield that much when struck, now that she thought about it. She swung up blind from the battle rage in her blood.

The figure parried her sword and gripped her wrist. "Pen, stop!"

She blinked, and her vision cleared, leaving her shaking, Tellus stood before her, just as stunned, with blood on his face. His sword was bloodied too.

Behind him, more villagers were catching up. The fire had caught in the trees. It was chasing them too.

"Go, run, go!" Tellus shouted, shoving Pen onward.

They ran again, oblivious of any sense of direction. The smoke caught up with them first, making it harder to breathe.

The trees ended again, but not at a clearing. A crevasse opened before them, with a river rushing below. Tellus skidded on loose gravel and nearly tumbled in. Pen managed to catch his belt and haul him the other way. He'd somehow gotten the belt on amongst the chaos, so he didn't lose his sheath.

"We have to jump," Pen said over the roaring flames and screaming villagers.

"What?"

She knew he'd heard her. "It's that or get roasted!"

The leaves above them started to smolder and catch fire.

"Fine!"

Tellus sheathed his sword and leapt. Pen withdrew her bloody swords and jumped after him. The smoke cleared as clean air rushed upward. She managed to get a lungful of air before the water swallowed her. She gasped as the current threw her along.

There was no up or down. Water pushed her from every angle, throwing her against rocks. She breached once and sucked for more air, but water half filled her mouth instead.

She went with the current, which eventually slowed. Finally, she was able to surface into blessed air. She spotted Tellus on the shore, and with the last of her strength she swam to him.

She staggered onto the land and laid on her back beside him, relishing the air free of smoke and water. Tellus was on his hands and knees, retching up water and coughing. He must have swallowed more than her. When he finally gained a breath, he sat down heavily beside her.

Pen straightened up and looked to the fire she had started. It had eaten a large section of the forest and was continuing to spread rapidly along the cliff's edge where they had jumped. They were safe at the bottom of a cliff that rose a hundred feet.

Then Pen remembered the girl.

"Samae," she said, turning to Tellus.

He had been watching the flames too, glad to be alive, but all happiness crumbled at the realization.

Pen wanted to run back in and find Samae, but there was no way back up the cliff.

Chapter Fourteen

They camped right there on the shore, too exhausted to move anywhere else.

"What do you think happens to the people they eat?" Tellus asked by the campfire that night.

Pen was quiet for a long time, honestly not sure. "Samae said they hadn't had visitors for a while. Maybe they hadn't found anyone to munch on these past few months."

"But if they did?" He sounded tired.

"Well… we know the headless bodies can't move. Maybe once they took enough off a person he couldn't fight back anymore. Can't exactly run without legs."

"Do you think they could feel their flesh cooking? Being… digested?"

"I don't bloody know!" She could only think of Samae burning.

At dawn Pen woke with cold sweats, probably due to falling asleep while still wet. Despite the fire she was cold, but she'd deal with it. The rising sun told them where east was, so they turned south again, back into the trees.

Pen couldn't stop thinking about Samae. She prayed the little girl knew the forest well enough to run to a safe place, but she was only six.

They walked somberly amongst the trees. It would be slower going without Demos and Zay, Pen missed the horses already, and they had no idea how wide the forest might be in this section. They could only do what they had been doing weeks before: walk south.

Pen couldn't get warm. She was now completely dry, and the air was brisk, but the cold had never bothered her until now. She followed close behind Tellus as he cut larger branches aside. She couldn't stop shivering, either, so she held her hands under her armpits, as if bracing from a snowstorm. She stumbled more often. The ground shifted beneath her feet, and sometimes the trees themselves would tilt. The world around her sounded muffled and wrong.

The world tilted again, and she fell to her knees but managed to catch herself. She stared at her hands, bewildered, as if her body had betrayed her. Tellus knelt before her and helped her stand again. She brushed off the dirt from her hands and she saw the cut on her palm. Her hand shook. The cut was swollen and dirty. The realization of what was happening made her heart stop.

"You're burning up." Tellus touched her forehead. "Are you feeling alright?"

"I didn't clean the blood."

"I'm sorry?" he asked.

"The blades I made. I didn't clean them when I drew the blood back in, and there was rust on the locks I opened," she explained, shaking.

"Oh! Can you draw that out?"

"I can only draw blood, not the dirt in it."

"What about the poisoned blood? Like snake venom?"

"It doesn't work like that. It's all mixed inside me!" She was shaking from fear now, along with the cold. She had come so close to Arch and Alard. She had no idea what the blood poisoning would do to her. She hoped it wouldn't leave her incapacitated like losing her head did, or leave her slowly rotting on the inside like King Aegeus

"It's okay," Tellus reassured her, "you'll get sick, but you won't die. I know you can fight this. Even without this undying curse, you're strong."

Her eyes snapped up to his.

"We can stop for the day. You should rest," he said.

"No, I can still walk." She didn't want to stop.

Tellus examined her closely. "If you're sure."

He let go of her shoulders, cautiously, as if she might fall again. She cleaned the wound as best as she could with their wineskin, which had thankfully been attached to Tellus's weapons belt, and continued on. Tellus stayed beside her to keep an eye on her condition.

Now that Pen knew she was sick, she kept somewhat better track of her footing. Her world still tilted, and her brain slowly filled with cotton. At one point she no longer had a sense of time, focusing so hard on her path. Tellus held her shoulder, and she leaned against him as they walked.

Eventually, Tellus stopped and set her down on a bed of moss. The light had changed and Pen realized the sun was setting.

Tellus knelt in front of her, hands on her shoulders, making sure she saw him. "You stay here. I'll light a fire and get some food."

He pressed the wineskin into her trembling hands and told her to drink as he left. She did, tentatively. Her stomach rolled a bit, but she managed to keep it down. She took one more swallow and lay down to wait for Tellus.

Arch stood before her. Pen reached out to touch him; she couldn't believe he was actually here. She was back in their cabin, back home. Chains rattled. She couldn't move. Her arms were spread apart with thick chains, her ankles were likewise shackled. She fought, calling to Arch. The chains rattled, and he didn't move. He stared at her. He wasn't glad to see her. He only stared, but his eyes weren't dead. They bored into her, hating her. Pen called to him again, begging for his help. The chains hurt. His hatred hurt more. She begged him to forgive her. He didn't reply. Blood started leaking from his eyes, nose, ears, mouth, and hairline. It dripped down his face from hundreds of pinpricks all over him. Pen screamed. The chains rattled. Arch moved then, shifting to show what he had been holding. Little Alard lay cradled in his arms. He was bleeding from wounds similar to his father's. His eyes stared at his mother too. They didn't show any happiness, nor did they show hatred. His eyes were dead. Pen screamed and screamed. The chains rattled, and the flesh on her wrists broke. Her own blood blossomed out, but she hadn't summoned it. It grew and spread around her like a spider's web of crimson. She screamed for Arch. He did nothing. The blood grew around her like a cage. It blocked out Arch's eyes, but she still felt the hate. She screamed for him not to leave her. He was gone. She saw a girl in his place. The girl's eyes were wrong, and she held a long bone. The chains rattled, and the blood suffocated her.

Pen woke, gasping. The air was damp and the sky above her was gray. She blinked. No, there was rock above her and she was dry. She was in a shallow cave; she could see the outside world was only a few feet away. It was raining. That was why it was damp, but there was a fire next to her, keeping her warm. Her dizziness had passed, though nausea played at the back of her throat, and her tongue was as dry as the wood in the fire. She needed water.

Tentatively, she propped herself up on one arm. The dizziness wasn't entirely gone after all, but it had receded. The wineskin was next to her. Taking it, she saw Tellus sitting by the entrance of their shallow cave, watching the rain. There was no wine, but he must have found a spring, because the skin was full of fresh water. Pen wanted to gulp it all down, but she took a small sip. When her stomach accepted it, she swallowed more. She sat up and Tellus's cloak pooled around her.

"Oh, thank the gods." Tellus moved to sit beside her. "How are you feeling?"

"Aright, I suppose," she replied, clutching the skin. "How long have I been asleep?"

"Three days."

"Well, that explains why I have to pee so badly."

Tellus chuckled and relaxed. Pen hadn't noticed at first, but he had been really concerned.

The rain wasn't heavy, so Pen went outside to take care of her business. When she came back Tellus stoked the fire and gave her a piece of squirrel meat.

"I guess the fever took over when I fell asleep," Pen said.

"You weren't just asleep; you were unconscious, and I had to carry you here when the rain started. On the second day you started screaming, and among those was Arch's name now and then. Nothing would calm you but I—" He stopped.

Pen waited, confused. After a moment he continued.

"I held you. It didn't help much, you were being… tortured by your dreams, I suppose, and I didn't know what else to do."

Pen didn't know how to reply, so she only said, "Thank you," but she meant it.

Tellus gave a half grin and shrugged it off. He didn't seem to know what to say either.

They stayed in the cave until the rain stopped.

Chapter Fifteen

After what felt like years, though it had only been a few weeks, Pen and Tellus reached the Acheron. Pen was taken aback by the sight of the river in the dusk. It was nearly a league across at this section. The waters trudged along slowly, but Pen knew the current was strongest in the middle. While most rivers would be edged with growth and life, the Acheron had only a sandy shore. The forest they came from ended several strides from the water, as if nature refused to grow too close to the water. Pen couldn't even find any animals or birds drinking from it. She wondered if there were any fish.

"We'll camp here for the night," Tellus said as he set down his pack.

Pen didn't argue but didn't feel calm either. She was standing with her back to him, watching the river. The back of her neck prickled like she was being watched. She turned and saw Tellus was watching the river too, looking as unnerved as she felt.

"I'll get the firewood." Tellus jumped a little as she spoke, and she suppressed a smile.

"I'll help you," he offered.

The fire provided relative warmth, but the breeze from the river was damp. During dinner of a skinny squirrel, Tellus said, "I can't even hear any bugs."

"I haven't seen a single bird," Pen added.

Tellus was quiet for a few moments. "This place isn't right."

"We're in the right place then." The sarcasm did nothing for her mood.

If the king was right they were closer to saving her son and Arch; all they had to do now was follow the Acheron upstream. There was no way of knowing how long it would take, since the source had never been found. The most avid adventurer would probably be turned back by the sheer uneasiness presented by the river. Pen couldn't deny she was excited by the mystery.

The trek was slow going without horses. Pen wondered if the horses would even have gotten this close to the river; perhaps they would have sensed danger and bolted. Most of the time, she and Tellus walked upstream in silence. Any conversation was clipped and awkward. The sense of unease grew like a fungus on her heart, but Pen refused to turn back. Her son was up ahead.

They walked for a fortnight. The presence of the river spread like a weed in her gut, and Tellus seemed equally unnerved.

The river narrowed in such tiny increments that Pen almost missed it, but it was true. Despite the unease, this sparked hope that they were getting closer.

Hills rose around them, with jagged rocks shooting up to the sky like teeth. It was as if giants had embedded them here. The rock gradually took over from the hills, and the grass died off. The Acheron was only about fifty paces wide here, flowing steadily.The nights were the worst part. They would continue to walk if the sky was clear and the moon let them see enough, but each time they stopped Pen could see the lights within the Acheron. Once, her father had been hired as a bodyguard for a merchant and they had traveled the sea for about a month. The lights in the river reminded her of schools of glowing fish in the ocean she had seen.

When they had started walking alongside the water, Pen had seen only one or two lights, but this close to the source there were dozens. The water was deeper and darker here, but Pen could see the slight green glow of something large swimming against the current. The figures of light varied in size, but they all swam in the same direction.

Pen knew Tellus had seen them too, but he made no comment; he wasn't one to state the obvious. She appreciated that in him. Turning to him now, she caught him watching the green lights. They cast him in a queasy glow, making him look sick. His worried expression didn't help.

"You okay?" Pen asked.

"I'm fine," he said.

The most common lie in the world, Pen would have said the same thing.

Eventually they came to a cliff face. The Acheron wound right into it. There was a small opening about five feet wide but only a few feet tall. It opened like a large mouth into the cliff face. Water poured out in a tiny waterfall, though the water didn't fill the opening, leaving dry space on both sides of the water, similar to the river bank Pen and Tellus had been walking on. The water fell a few feet before reaching the river bed. The green figures followed the water effortlessly from the river up the waterfall and were swallowed by the rock mouth.

"You have to be joking," Tellus scoffed. It was the most he'd said all day.

Pen would fit easily into the opening, but it would be awkward for him.

"I'll go scout out the inside, then help you in," she offered. She made to climb into the little cave.

Tellus gripped her arm. "No, you don't. We're going to wait for a new day."

"The sun hasn't even set yet," she protested, pulling away. "There's hours of daylight left."

"I'm not going in there until we've had a day of rest. The gods know we need it."

Her son was in there. "We've come this far, and now you're stalling!"

"Rushing in could get us killed," he countered.

"So we just wait? We've reached the source of the Acheron, and you want to wait?"

"Your family isn't going anywhere, if they are even in there. I hate to make him suffer any longer than necessary, but even Aegeus can wait one more day for us to rest. Then we can go down there with fresh heads. I don't plan on encountering Nyx or Maniodes half asleep."

The rational part of her mind knew he was right. The irrational part wanted to rush in and find her husband and their boy. She took a breath and heeded Tellus. They set a tiny fire with the half dead bushes; there were no trees.

Pen didn't know what Tellus was doing. She sat on the rocks, unable to look away from the green lights disappearing into the cave mouth.

Darkness had fallen over them like an oppressive blanket. There was no moon tonight, making the glow of the lights more prominent in the dark. Pen looked over her shoulder to Tellus; he'd fallen asleep beside their measly fire. How he was even able to sleep here, she had no idea. The air made her skin crawl. Everything felt wrong about this place.

Pen got up and approached the cave mouth. The bottom edge of the cave came to about her waist, and the glowing lights flowed into it as though being swallowed. She peered inside. There was nothing but blackness; even the lights simply disappeared once past the rock. She reached out but found no obstruction. She felt nothing as her hand and arm were seemingly swallowed by the black wall.

She pulled her arm back and looked to Tellus. If travelers who came this way never returned, this black wall might be why. They were about to enter the land of the dead, and it made a strange kind of sense that they couldn't leave. If Aegeus was right that she could travel here unhindered because of her magic, then Tellus probably wasn't immune. He could be trapped down there.

She turned back to the entrance. There was no stopping him, and he most certainly knew of the danger anyway, and yet he came. The rational part of her mind told her to wait for him to wake, to get some sleep herself.

But the irrational part won. Pen climbed inside the blackness, careful not to touch the water.

Blackness swallowed her and she couldn't see for a moment, but that passed quickly. The mouth of the cave was only about a foot deep, but after that point Pen was able to stand. Where she expected a low rock ceiling there was nothing. The rock above the opening ran up a sheer wall and disappeared into shadows. She stood on a gravelly shore beside the Acheron. The river was only a few paces wide here and flowed quickly. It took a moment for her to understand what she was seeing. She stood at the top of a hill, where the cave mouth was letting the water out, and it was flowing up that hill from a huge valley below her. The green lights continued to swim downhill, against the current.

The valley was so wide that Pen couldn't see the other end or sides. There wasn't exactly a horizon either. There was no stone above her, like a normal cave, only soft blackness, as if this underground valley had its own sky made of shadows. Where the horizon should have been, the sky and ground melded and disappeared.

She could see movement in the distance. It looked like figures moving slowly in a grey fog. It seemed that none of the figures did anything other than walk. They didn't do anything threatening, at least to each other. Pen made sure the wound on her hand was open but clean, in case she needed anything.

Entranced, Pen began to walk down the hill and into the valley. The ground gave way to dry, brittle grass. There were trees, sparse and dead. The Acheron divided the valley in half like a spine, and several smaller rivers branched off it like ribs. Every so often a green light would break off from the main group and follow one of these smaller rivers. She couldn't see what determined their paths.

As she descended the hill, she saw the dead. There were thousands, possibly millions, of people walking about. Young and old, rich and poor, criminals and saints, warriors and peasants and kings all ended up here. Their clothing was the easiest way to determine the general status of a person, but Pen knew those were only assumptions. Still, it was easy to tell the well dressed, if overweight, man from the thin beggar dressed in a ripped tunic. Regardless of what they looked like in life now they walked, eyes dead and bored, with all color leached out of them. They looked like greasy, gray husks.

Unnerved, Pen walked among them, seeing them, but they didn't see her. They ignored her as she passed. They treated her like any other shade; it made her cold thinking that she could easily be one of them. Some of them were sitting against the trees and rocks. Some even laid on the ground. The ones who walked avoided her, but some ran into each other. Nothing happened; they only passed through each other with little wisps of gray trailing behind them. The ones on the ground were constantly being walked on, or rather through, but paid the intruders no heed. They could only stare blankly up to their velvety sky, if it could be called a sky.

Pen came to the first fork of the Acheron. The main river had widened again, but its branches were still narrow. Pen noted that were rocks sticking out of the river on some sections. The lights flowed around them effortlessly.

Not wanting to disturb the water or the lights within, Pen hopped to one rock, then another. A dead tree on the other bank had branches that extended towards her; she was able to grab a thick branch and climb hand over hand to the other side. She continued to follow the main spine of the Acheron, which provided the only real sense of direction.

Pen realized that even though she had made it all the way to the source of the Acheron in the living world, then reached Skiachora, she had no idea what to do next to find Nyx. She made a quick mental correction. The Acheron still flowed beside her; she had found where it left this world and entered her own, but she hadn't found the *exact* source.

Keeping the green light of the Acheron in view, she veered off toward a rock outcrop. Hundreds of the dead sat here, staring into nothing. Pen stopped in front of an older woman dressed in rich clothing and a gold necklace, and sat beside a teenage boy dressed in rags who looked like he hadn't bathed in years. Two people different in every way had ended up in the same place. She knelt in front of the old woman, but the elder didn't see anything; her dead eyes were like glass. The boy's eyes were the same, though he blinked. It was slow and tired, as if it were more of a remembered action, and the body did it automatically.

Pen realized that these creatures couldn't be considered as having physical bodies. The shades were definitely people, but she couldn't touch them, and their real bodies were buried above them.

Pen left them. Crossing another stream, she came to a small grove of six dead trees. The shades here were the same as everywhere else. Another smaller grouping of rocks was the same.

She crossed the third spring, and looking back she couldn't see the hills that rose around them, or the little cave mouth. It was cold down here, though even without the chill the isolation and shades of the dead would have been enough to make the bravest tremble. Pen swallowed that fear and kept going.

A tall tree loomed out of the dark. The leafless branches clawed upward like skeletal fingers. The two figures at the base of it were Arch and Alard.

Pen froze, unable to move or breathe for a long time. They were a fair distance away, and the shades passed between them, but she recognized her husband by his mop of hair. The way he sat slumped against the tree was reminiscent of how he died. The child beside him had similar hair. Eventually her legs did let her move. She sprinted to them and fell to her knees beside them.

Arch sat with his back to the tree trunk. His head was bowed slightly, and his heavy lidded eyes gazed at, or perhaps through, the ground between his feet. Alard was close by, curled up beside a rock. He was laying on his side similar to how he died. Pen wanted to pick him up and never let go. Neither moved nor even breathed. Only then did Pen realize the wounds she had inflicted were gone. But little Alard's eyes were as dead as they were in her dreams, staring through her.

Those dreams woke the memories, and she shook as she relived the moment.

Dirt clung under Pen's nails as she dug at the weeds in the small garden. She enjoyed working here, but the heat of the day was taking all enjoyment out it. Pausing for a moment, she took a swing from the skinful of water at her belt.

"Alard," she called.

A little boy, just over his third year, hopped out of the sandy patch in the grass. His clothes were covered in filth, about as much as her hands, and her heart swelled with pride. Getting the mud stains out later would be tough, though.

"Hi, Mama!" he squealed as he reached her.

Pen took a handkerchief and cleaned most of the dust from his face, replying, "Hello, sweetheart."

She pressed the skin into his hands. "Drink up."

The boy took the skin and drank; he needed it too. Pen noticed his black hair plastered to his forehead like hers. She'd keep a closer eye on him in this heat. He handed the skin back once he'd had his fill.

"When's Papa coming back?" he asked.

"Later today, when he's finished at the market," she replied.

"Why is he at the market?"

"To buy nails for the roof."

"Why?"

"Because it's old. Now why don't you go back and play in the sand." She loved him, but the constant stream of questions wouldn't stop unless he was distracted.

"Okay!" He trotted off to the sandy patch, then called back, "Come and play."

"Not now, sweetheart. I need to finish the garden so we can eat later."

"Okay." He sat and continued drawing in the sand.

A couple of hours later, as the sun was touching the treetops of their clearing, Pen glanced out of the window of their cabin after cleaning out the fireplace. Alard was in his room, playing with blocks his father made him. Pen saw her husband through the window approaching the porch. She wiped her hands on her apron, staining it further, then opened the door for Arch.

After her father died Pen had traveled alone. During a bad winter she had stopped at a village, a tiny place called Malliae, and she'd had every intention of leaving when the snows melted. That was where she met Arch. She had stayed a little longer, not being very sociable, but she grew close to him. She planned to leave in the summer but stayed because Arch had asked her to. A few months later, Alard was on his way.

Arch blinked in surprise as the door opened, but his eyes lit up when he saw Pen. He dropped his pack onto the table and took Pen in his arms, kissing her lightly. Her heart beat a little faster as she breathed in the scent of him: horses and grass.

Arch smiled. "Well, hello to you too, m'lady."

"How was town?"

"Busy for the heat today, but most of the venders were practically asleep. I could only get ten nails."

"Only ten?" Pen asked, genuinely surprised.

"The coins didn't amount to much."

Disappointment bloomed in her heart, not at Arch, but the fact they couldn't afford more than a handful of nails.

They always got by fine, but she still worried about emergencies.

Arch must have seen the worry in her expression. He held her shoulders and said, "That's probably all I will need anyway. It wasn't a big hole."

Pen smiled into his gray eyes; they always reminded her of a soft rain. "You'll figure it out."

Arch kissed her again. "So where's the little man?"

"In his room playing."

"Great." He let her go and strode to Alard's room. "Anything good for dinner?"

"Duck," she replied.

Arch grimaced a little. "Again?"

Pen shrugged and shooed him away so she could start dinner.

She woke that night to a pleasant, cool draught, but something was off. Her sleep addled mind took a moment to clear before she realized her wrists were hurting. It was just a dull ache that woke her, which was unusual. They had never bothered her before. Maybe it was too much work in the garden or from cleaning the fireplace. Her father told her that Mother had pains in her fingers as she grew older, and she knew joints started to hurt as one aged, but Pen was only twenty one. Worried that it might be setting in early, she curled up beside Arch and tried to sleep.

The ache did not dissipate but grew. She was wide awake at this point, with Arch snoring softly on his side, facing away from her. Moving her hands to loosen them didn't help, nor did rolling her wrists or rubbing them. She sat up on the straw mattress. The ache grew to agonizing pain, and now her wrists started to itch.

The skin of the softest part itched terribly on both wrists. Pen scratched, but it did not ebb. She threw back the blanket and left the bedroom. There was a pitcher of water on the table in the small kitchen. She pushed both her hands inside it. The cool water helped distract her for a minute. Removing her hands caused the pain and itch to flare up almost immediately. Grunting in frustration, she dried her hands. Red marks from her nails marked her skin now. She knew she had to stop before there was blood, but the itch was maddening.

She sat at the table and gripped her hands together, forcing herself not to scratch. Tiny pinpricks of blood marked where her nails had broken the skin. The itch felt like thousands of tiny bugs were trying to break out of her skin.

Her will broke; she scratched and dug at her skin. She wanted to cry out but managed to control the urge, not wanting to wake the others. She should wake Arch; at least he might have an idea or get her to stop.

Blood broke to the surface. Her fingers quickly turned slick and red, smearing it halfway up her forearm. She couldn't stop; both wrists bled but the itch wouldn't stop. She stood and paced, not realizing she'd knocked over the chair. The blood dripped, but the itch wouldn't stop; it even overpowered the pain. She scratched and scratched and scratched.

There was a voice at the edge of her hearing. She ignored it. The itch shrank her world to nothing but the mad irritation. The voice sounded again but louder.

Suddenly Arch was in front on her, having taken hold of her shoulders.

"What on earth are you doing?" He stared in horror at her hands.

He took them and forced them apart. Blood welled from the ripped wounds. Her hands twitched and fought against his grip.

"It won't stop," Pen managed to say.

"What won't stop?" Arch's voice was soft with concern.

"Itches," was all she could whisper. It had driven her mad for a moment.

"Papa?"

Pen snapped back to reality. Her son stood in the doorway of his room, rubbing a sleepy eye. He blinked and stared at the pool of blood under his mother.

"Go back to your room, little man, Mama's alright." Arch's voice broached no argument.

The only thing Pen could say to describe what happened next was that her blood exploded. It sprang from her wounds outward in all directions. There was no time to scream, but she noticed how it mostly avoided her, only painting her red. The itch was gone, but her blood now sprouted from her wrists like long hair swirling underwater. It turned into thousands of thin tendrils that filled the house. They stayed only for a second then shrank back into her wrists. Pen hadn't realized how dizzy she was until the blood was back in its proper place. The pain was gone, but the gashes still decorated her skin.

Struggling to get her bearings, Pen was about to tell Arch that the pain and itch were gone, but then she saw him. He had been thrown across the room in front of her. Thousands of punctures dotted his face, neck, torso, and limbs. Even his eyes bled from where they were struck. He sat slumped against the far wall, staring blankly. A thick line of more blood ran on the wall from where his head had struck it several feet above him. His skull was broken.

Pen couldn't breathe. Looking to where her son had been, she saw he had been thrown too. He lay on his side in a spreading pool of crimson, his beautiful dark eyes dead.

Tears streaked down her face, and she struggled to gain air. She went to touch Alard's cheek, but her fingers passed through him. She wrenched her hand back as if she'd struck him by accident.

She knelt with her dead family and wept.

She didn't want to leave them; she could hardly feel her legs from kneeling so long. They didn't even know she was there. She forced herself to stand. Her legs wouldn't obey at first, but she moved. She stood beside them.

"I'll get you out of here," she whispered. "I'll bring you back and everything will be alright again."

She left them waiting.

Pen didn't explore anywhere else; she followed the Acheron upriver into the darkness. The dead wandered past her.

The scenery gradually changed. The dead trees and rocks became scarcer, and the dead didn't roam as freely here. The Acheron stopped branching, and there were fewer lights in the water. Most of the green lights had followed one fork or another, but some remained this far upstream.

Something large loomed out of the darkness. At first Pen assumed it was some kind of building, but it was hard to tell. As she drew closer she saw that it was bigger than she had at first thought, and made of crafted stone. The ground suddenly fell away before her, and she watched as the green lights dropped into nothingness beneath her. She could see nothing below but the flow of the river rushing upward in a reverse waterfall. This was the source of the Acheron. She didn't know what was down there, but knew she couldn't follow it.

She looked back up at the immense castle. She had no idea whether it floated over this chasm or sat atop its own cliff or pillar. There were no walls, but a fence of black iron ringed the land mass on which the castle stood. The carved stone she had seen was a staircase stretching from the land above her down to where she stood. At the top of the stone stairs was an iron gate. The stairs descended, split in two, and ended on either side of the Acheron.

From this angle she couldn't see much of Maniodes's castle but what she could see was daunting. The stone was weathered and the shingles on the towers were chipped. There were several towers haphazardly surrounding a larger one in the center. There didn't appear to be any order to the design of the castle. Two of the towers were missing their steep roofs, as if they had been snapped off by a giant. Other towers had chunks of stone missing, and one was leaning dangerously to one side like a broken spine, probably the remnants of an old war. The cold stone left Pen feeling small and alone. She wished she'd waited for Tellus, but it was too late now.

Pen had been traveling along the left shore of the river, so she climbed the left staircase.

The castle stood before her now on the other side of the iron fence. Pen rattled the iron but the gate didn't give. She expected as much, and wondered whether she could make some contraption from her blood to get her over. The courtyard beyond the gate was flat, with dead grass and a couple of dead trees. A gravel road led from the gate to the castle door several yards away. She could hear the Acheron roaring below her feet, but still couldn't tell if the castle was floating or not. She wouldn't be surprised if it was.

The castle of Maniodes appeared destroyed, as if damaged in a siege and never repaired. Cracks ran up the walls, and the windows were shattered. Most of the crenellations remained, but were chipped, and several were missing, like a jaw missing some teeth. The great doors were rotting.

As she watched, the doors opened and two soldiers walked out. They walked along the gravel road toward her. She had no place to hide. She hadn't exactly been stealthy in coming here and gawking at the place, so they must have seen her the moment she arrived. Perhaps they had known of her arrival as soon as she had entered the little cave mouth.

The soldiers come closer, and Pen saw they were actually skeletons in armor. Her heart rate quickened, but she stood her ground. Unlike the shades, they seemed conscious of their actions. They opened the gate and held it aside for her, then waited, watching her with empty eye sockets. Pen entered the courtyard. Under their empty gazes and the amongst the cold stone Pen felt fear creeping into her veins. She forced it back and stood her ground. The skeleton soldiers closed the gate and fell in step behind her. They didn't touch her, but she knew where they wanted her to go. She walked up the gravel road to the rotting castle.

The doors opened, seemingly by themselves. As Pen stepped inside she saw two more skeleton soldiers holding the doors. She found herself in a vast entrance hall. On either side were doors, and on the second floor she could see balconies on either side, and archways and pillars. Everything was made of the same dark gray stone. Fissures ran through the blocks of stone, and in some places the mortar was as thin as spider's silk. Other sections were lined with cracks that ran to the ceiling and were wide enough for two horses to pass abreast. The place looked like it was about to crumble.

Above her hung a chandelier made of polished silver that webbed outward. Banners hung on the walls, providing the only decoration. There were red, with the sigil stitched in black: a crossed scythe and dagger.

The palace was empty except for Pen and the skeletons. One of them approached and pointed down the hall, its joints clicking. There stood a pair of double doors similar to the outer entrance. The wood was black, as if the doors had been burned, but they were intact.

Pen approached the burned doors, thinking of Arch and Alard. The doors swung open to reveal a great hall. The walls were the same as the rest of the castle. The pillars holding up the tall ceiling were wider than the oldest trees she'd seen. Torches ringed the pillars, providing light, but it wasn't the only source. There was a hole in the roof with stone and wooden beams jutting out like teeth. A soft gray light lit a spot on the floor.

Pen stepped onto a purple rug that ran all the way to a dais, upon which were two thrones made of shiny black rock. She had never seen that much obsidian in one piece. Both thrones were empty.

This was bizarre. After walking all this way to find Nyx, she was led to an empty hall?

There was a single door behind the thrones. It opened a crack. Pen could hear voices. As she watched the door, a man stepped through but looked back as if waiting for another. He was young, with straight black hair that hung to his shoulders. He wore a black leather tunic and black trousers with a cape lined with rich white fur.

"She's here watching me right now," he said to whoever was behind the door.

Pen heard a woman's voice respond but couldn't make out the words. She sounded annoyed.

"Then leave them behind," the man said. He looked back to Pen, smiled, and shrugged apologetically.

A woman stepped out. Her hair was deep red and hung well past her waist. She wore a black, sleeveless silk dress with a spider's web design that started at her shoulder and spread across the whole dress.

"Sorry about the delay," the woman called to Pen. The couple came forward, passed the thrones, and stepped off the dais to meet her in the middle of the hall. Pen noticed then that she was barefoot.

"Shoes can be so restrictive," the woman said dismissively.

"My name is Dagger," the man said, "and this is my lady wife, Scythe."

Pen stammered honestly, not sure how to proceed. Were they royalty? Mediators? They didn't seem human, something about them felt wrong.

"Like the weapons?" she asked eventually.

Dagger nodded. "Yes, exactly. And you must be Pen?"

"Yes."

"Oh, good, I'm glad you were able to make it here." Scythe said, smiling. "Though we are surprised at your presence."

"Shouldn't Maniodes be here? He's the ruler of Skiachora."

"We overthrew him decades ago," Dagger said.

"Don't worry about it," Scythe said. "Why did you come?"

Pen was shocked these two could just dethrone a god. "I came to find out why people can no longer die. People are suffering from sickness and horrific wounds, but nothing can release them."

"We're the rulers of the dead, yes, but it is not our job to help them die." Dagger sounded annoyed all of a sudden. Pen sensed immediately that he was holding something back.

"You must know where Nyx is, right? She provides you with those… those souls," Pen protested.

Dagger just stared at her, dumbfounded. Scythe looked equally confused.

"You're the one who stole her," Dagger said acidly, "and you dare come here demanding our help when you kidnapped our friend? We only know that she went to collect you months ago."

"What?" Pen nearly laughed, it was so absurd.

"You don't remember?" Scythe asked. She appeared upset, too, but controlled it better.

"Remember what? That I somehow kidnapped a bloody goddess?"

"My lord?" a voice behind Pen interrupted.

Pen spun and her hand went to her weapon. A man stood there, gray like the other shades, but there was life in his eyes.

"The sentries have found the other one."

"They brought him here?" Scythe asked the messenger.

"Yes, my lady."

Dagger only glared at Pen. It made a chill run down her spine but she stared back, challenging him to do something. What he had accused her of was ridiculous.

"Thank you," Scythe said. "Bring him in."

The gray man bowed and left through the burned doors. A pair of skeleton soldiers escorted in another gray man. Pen froze. It was Tellus. All color had leached from his hair and eyes, even his skin. He was gray, like the shades, but more solid. He was breathing and his eyes were alive. His eyes showed pain, and every step was like a lurch forward. The soldiers departed. Tellus stood hunched over, forcing air into his lungs. Pen went to touch him, to see if there was anything she could do, but her hand passed through his arm as it had with Alard. But where Alard didn't react, Tellus looked like he wanted to scream.

Dagger and Scythe looked equally concerned for him. Scythe placed her hands on his shoulders. Pen didn't know what she did, but she could touch him, and it seemed to draw out the gray. His color came back and he fell to his knees, gasping and clutching his chest.

Pen knelt and helped him stand. For a moment he leaned on her for support, then he straightened. His breathing seemed easier now.

"What happened?" Pen asked.

"I woke up and you were gone. It wasn't hard to guess where you had gone, so I climbed into the cave and… and it felt like something wanted to tear out of my body but couldn't. Part of me actually wanted to crawl into the Acheron down here with those lights." He noticed the two before them. "Who are you?"

"I'm Scythe, and this is Dagger. We're the rulers here," Scythe explained.

Tellus glanced beyond them to the thrones.

"Those chairs are not comfortable enough to sit in for long," Dagger said.

"That was your soul, by the way," Scythe said. "Any mortal who wanders in here instantly loses it and is stuck here. Once someone enters, they can't leave."

"Then why was I unaffected?" Pen asked. She hadn't felt any of what Tellus described.

"Because you're one of us, at least in part. You're the Blood Warrior."

Tellus turned to Pen. "Aegeus was right. You are a demigod."

"Both of my parents were mortal. My mother died in childbirth," she protested.

"That's not important right now," Dagger interrupted. He asked Tellus, "I assume you're here for the same reason she is?"

"Aye," Tellus replied, "we need your help for the dying people above, or at least lead us to Nyx, given the myths of her. If this place exists, she must as well."

Dagger chuckled but still looked furious. "What makes you even think we care about the people before they're dead?"

Tellus was taken aback. Pen stayed quiet, watching Dagger, wondering if his previous comment about demigods was a trick.

"You're gods, aren't you?" Tellus demanded, growing furious too. "How can you not care for your people?"

Scythe joined in Dagger's laughter. "The dead here are in our charge. They are our people."

"Nyx would know, then, take us to her," Tellus said.

"You do not order us."

Pen grew cold again at Dagger's voice.

Scythe looked insulted by Tellus's demands, too, but she smirked, as though she was watching a puppy growling. Dagger looked ready to tear out their throats.

"We cannot take you to Nyx," Scythe said. "We don't know where she is."

"You must have some way to find her. Some hints," Tellus said. "Please."

"We don't," Dagger replied though gritted teeth. "But *she* does."

Dagger and Scythe turned back to Pen, watching her reaction.

"Wait, what?" Tellus turned on Pen too. "What are they talking about?"

Pen shrugged. It had to be some kind of riddle. "I don't know. How can I *kidnap* a goddess?"

"You don't remember anything, do you?" Scythe asked.

"I'm sure I'd remember if I had met Nyx and lived."

Dagger instantly softened. The rage melted away. He turned to Scythe and said, "Her mind broke."

"My mind is fine, thank you."

"Hold on," Tellus said. "Pen, you know where Nyx is? This entire time you held her somewhere? Is that what started the curse?"

"I didn't!"

Tellus looked like she'd betrayed him. She hated that look in his eyes. She wasn't angry at him for it, but the disappointment was deep enough to drown in.

"I didn't," she said again, not looking away from his green eyes.

He studied her face, then nodded. He believed her, and she could breathe again.

"She did," Scythe said, no longer ready to strike them, but gentle. "She just doesn't remember it."

"If she said she didn't—"

"Any witness account can be flawed, Captain," she said. Pen assumed she used his title to remind him of his job. He no doubt dealt with witness accounts all the time. "But we can help her remember."

Pen growled, "I'm not crazy."

"No, you're not, you're grieving," Scythe replied softly.

"Your loved ones, Pen, your family, they died about three months ago?" Dagger asked.

What did that have to do with it? "Yes."

"What happened afterward?"

"What? Nothing, I buried them and left, I… I couldn't stay there."

"What makes you think Pen took Nyx?" Tellus asked.

"Because she was the last person Nyx went to retrieve," Dagger explained. "Before that, she had been spending the day with us. She's rather good at darts."

They didn't make sense. Why would Nyx have to *retrieve* Pen?

"But," Tellus began, and Pen could see he was thinking the same thing as her, "why go to her if she wasn't dying?"

"She was," Scythe said. "We aren't sure how she was doing it, but Nyx mentioned she was killing herself."

"No," Pen refused the notion, "no that's… what? No."

"We heard those words from Nyx herself before she went to you." Dagger shrugged. "Then she was gone."

"No!" She didn't want to think of that time after they died. She couldn't, she refused. Her mind tried to go there anyway, but encountered a lonely emptiness. "No."

"Pen?" Tellus reached for her as if to steady her.

"I didn't do this! I didn't kill myself! I'm standing right here, aren't I?"

"Something happened when you met her," Scythe said, "but only you know what."

Pen was shaking, she couldn't think back.

Scythe came forward to comfort her, but Pen flinched away.

"It's alright, Pen," Dagger said. "You're not the first person whose mind has slipped. Sometimes it happens to protect yourself. I've dealt with it myself in a way."

"You have?" Tellus asked.

"My mother killed me in a period of insanity. Whenever she was questioned about it later, she couldn't remember, and when she was lucid she would ask for me."

"You have a mother?"

"That's not the point right now," Dagger said. "Scythe, do you think she can handle Mnemosyne?"

"I don't know, I don't think she can even hear us anymore," Scythe replied.

"Pen?" Tellus was very concerned now.

"I *can* hear you," she said directly to Scythe, forcing the shaking to stop but failing. "I'm not crazy."

"I know," Scythe said gently. "We can help you remember what happened."

"There's nothing to remember."

"But if there is? It could lead you to Nyx. And we would get our friend back."

Finding Nyx would mean getting closer to her family, her son.

"Fine. What do I do?"

"Come with me." Scythe went to take her arm, but Pen pulled away again.

Scythe shrugged and led them outside to the courtyard. Thankfully, Tellus stayed close to Pen. He was a foundation she could count on. Dagger followed close behind. Scythe took them around the castle to a rose garden. There were more thorns than roses in the bushes, and streaming through the garden was a little river that flowed from beneath the castle to the iron fence and disappeared into the chasm.

"This river is Mnemosyne: Memory," Scythe explained.

"Lethe runs on the other side of the castle," Dagger continued. "The river of forgetfulness."

Scythe left the group and crossed to an iron table and chairs. On the table was a tea set made of ivory with black designs of spiders. She picked up one of the cups and returned, filling it with water from the river.

"All you need to do is drink." Scythe held up the cup.

Pen stared at the cup as if it were filled with urine. This was ridiculous; her mind wouldn't break on her, and these people were lying. All she had to do to prove them wrong was drink the water, because nothing would happen. Why didn't she want to? She found that she couldn't move her arms to take it. It felt like lead was weighing them down. She wanted to prove to them she wouldn't remember anything new, because nothing happened. Her heart beat like she'd run a mile. Her hands still shook, no matter how much she clenched them.

"Pen," Tellus said, "if you know where Nyx is, we need you to drink this."

His voice roused her, and she moved without trying to think. She took the cup from Scythe and held it, still watching the water like it was poison.

She held on to the trembling cup as tightly as she held onto Arch and Alard in her heart. She downed the water in one gulp.

Chapter Sixteen

The day was beautiful; it wasn't as hot as yesterday, with the comforting breeze. Pen's heart couldn't be blacker. She couldn't even feel anymore, but she knew her body ached from working and digging all night. She didn't care; she might pass out, but she had one more thing to do. One more task, then everything would be alright again, and they would be together. Pen knelt facing the fresh graves, one large and one small, under their willow tree, knife in hand.

She brought the blade up to the soft spot under her left ear on her neck and pulled. Her heart kicked with panic, the first drip of different emotion she'd felt since she killed them. She felt the thin flesh of her throat cut cleanly open. It stung yet felt warm.

Pen blinked. There was a girl in front of her. There was no puff of smoke or flash of godly light; she simply existed there. She was small, maybe ten years of age, her form swimming in a black robe. Her black hair hung free, a few strands playing in the beautiful breeze. What was most striking were her eyes and what she held. Her eyes were wrong. Where the color and black pupil should have been, there were only white discs, while the whites of her eyes were black. She clutched a long bone in one hand. Pen had no doubt that the bone was human.

She could feel her blood wanting to leak out of the wound on her neck. She almost wanted to let it, but her new power allowed her to control the flow and keep it from spreading. She kept herself from dying, facing the Goddess of Death herself.

"Bring them back." she said, her voice rough from the gash.

Nyx cocked her head in surprise. Pen smirked; in the myths Nyx took the souls of the dying and released them from pain. At the end of every story the victim was always willing to go with her. Pen was not.

Nyx shook her head sadly. "I cannot do that." Though her body was a child's, her voice was that of a grown woman.

"You can," Pen insisted. "I've heard the stories. You take their souls but you can give them back."

"I can't. I don't know why you mortals made up that part of the story, but I can't."

She was lying. Pen knew she was lying, she *had* to be lying. "You're lying."

"I'm not, Pen," Nyx said. "You buried them yourself, you know this. The dead cannot come back."

"You're lying!" Desperation made her heart kick again.

Nyx came forward and knelt in front of Pen, looking into her face, no doubt dirty and tear streaked, with white eyes.

"I cannot bring them back, Pen, but I can help you." Nyx held up the bone. "You can join them."

The bone was how Nyx took and carried the souls of people; all they had to do was touch it, and they always did willingly. Pen wondered if Arch and Alard were inside that bone. She wanted to be sick.

She wanted to break that bone.

"Let go of your power, Blood Warrior." Nyx's voice was soothing, intoxicating. "It's alright, the pain will end."

She offered the bone.

Pen reached up and let her blood flow. It struck Nyx in the chest, lifting her off her feet and pinning her to the willow tree. A tendril of blood grabbed the bone and wrenched it from Nyx's hand.

Pen stood, weak from the blood loss, but the desperation to be reunited with her family gave her strength. She held one hand out toward Nyx, holding her there. Blood covered the goddess's robes like sticky sap. Pen had the blood sprout manacles to pin Nyx's arms to the tree as well. The tendril that held the bone hovered nearby, not touching Pen's flesh.

Her theory had been right. All of the people in the myths who touched the bone did it with their hand, their skin. Pen could hold things now, not with her hands but with her will channeled through her blood.

"Release me!" At Nyx's shout, the tree shook and loose dirt fell from the fresh graves.

"Bring Arch and Alard back," Pen demanded.

"It's physically impossible for them to come back! I will punish you for this, mortal!"

Pen moved her hand to point at the object she had left by Alard's grave. Another tendril of blood picked up the long pine box and placed it in her hand. She removed the lid of the tiny coffin. She'd crudely made it of spare wood before burying her husband and son.

"No," Nyx said.

Pen willed her blood to move the goddess's bone into the little coffin. Then she closed the lid.

Nyx screamed, and the sky darkened. She disappeared, screaming in agony, becoming a form of thick smoke. The smoke was sucked into the pine box with the bone.

Nyx was gone.

Pen drew most of her blood back inside her but used some to hold the pine coffin closed as she nailed it shut with the nails Arch bought from town. She then buried it between Arch and Alard under the willow tree.

Pen's father had been right; there was a way to trap the goddess forever. She didn't feel better, though. The goddess had won. Pen would be punished and suffer a fate worse than death.

She would live.

Pen lowered the cup, defeated. Oddly enough, the shaking had stopped. Dread sank into her gut; she had started the curse of undying. The cup was empty now, but she couldn't look away.

"So how long do we wait?" she heard Tellus ask. "What happens now?"

"We don't have to wait at all," Dagger answered. "It's instantaneous."

Pen felt Tellus at her side. "Pen? Did it work?"

"I started this," she managed.

"Do you know where Nyx is?"

Pen addressed only Tellus, telling him everything. She told them how she had sealed Nyx away because she couldn't save her family.

Tellus's expression changed from concerned to studiously blank. Pen knew he must have felt cheated or betrayed; he'd been traveling to fix this curse with the very person who caused it.

"How did you know to seal Nyx away like that?" Scythe asked quietly.

"My father told me about it. He always told me stories of the gods and their deeds when I was little."

Dagger asked Tellus, "Did you know about that? Have you heard that in any myth?"

"No, I haven't," he replied. "I didn't know it was even possible."

"Mortals are not supposed to know how to do that. So how did your father learn that detail?"

"He never told me where he heard the stories." Pen shrugged. "I'd assumed it was common knowledge."

"It's not, nor should it ever be." Dagger turned on Pen. "If you reveal it, it will pit all of the immortals against you."

She believed him, and she was already damned enough. "I won't share it."

"Nor will I," Tellus promised.

"Of course not," Scythe said dismissively. "You will release Nyx."

"On one condition," Pen said steadfastly.

Tellus glared at her. "This is not the time."

"You want your son and husband back." Dagger sounded almost bored.

"Yes."

"And I take it this is part of the 'gods will owe us a favor if we grant them one' nonsense?"

The steel in Pen's spine had deteriorated after she drank the water of Mnemosyne. Now Dagger's voice made her want to cower. She held on to Arch and Alard with nothing but stubbornness.

"Give them back to me, and I will release Nyx."

"She wasn't lying before. She couldn't bring them back, and neither can we. Once the dead enter this place, they can't leave."

Pen wanted to find a dark corner that matched her black heart, and give in to the pain, but she stayed put.

"They are safe here," Scythe said.

"There's nothing here!" Pen couldn't stop thinking of the dead eyes of her family.

"But they don't know that."

"They don't know anything!"

"Is that a bad thing? They no longer feel pain."

"They can't feel anything."

"Argue all you want, Pen. You can't change the rules."

Any further argument died in Pen's throat. Tellus's hand touched her shoulder. Pen wanted to scream, but didn't.

"Keep in mind that they are in our care. They can't leave, but we can give them back their consciousness. They can't leave, but they will know they are dead, and how they got here, for eternity." Scythe's voice shattered Pen as though she were made of fragile glass. "Unless you save Nyx from that pine box."

"Is that necessary?" Tellus sounded defeated too.

Neither responded.

If Arch and Alard woke up but couldn't leave, they'd still be wandering with the dead but aware of it. She might be able to talk to them, and Arch would understand; he knew she loved him. He would know it was an accident, but that would mean subjecting him to horrible knowledge and not being able to do anything about it. And Alard would be terrified. They would explain what they could to him, but he would be a three year old boy stuck at that age, with ghosts constantly surrounding him. She couldn't do that to them.

Then she thought about Aegeus with his cancer and Narciso with his infected wound. She thought of Samae from the forest and the cannibals they burned. And the heads kept by the Ragged Wolves. What agony were they in?

Death was naturally terrifying, but it did provide a natural release and peace. It was part of nature that could not be avoided. And Pen had taken that release away from everyone; she had corrupted nature itself. It shouldn't be sought after, but it can never be forgotten or ignored. And that was the one thing these shades had; they were remembered by loved ones above.

"I'll release Nyx," Pen said.

"Good," Dagger replied. "As a sign of good faith, we can take you there directly. The parts of the stories about us appearing out of thin air? That's true, and we can do it to others."

"So you'll transport us instantly to Pen's home? That would have been useful getting here," Tellus said. Despite his joke, he sounded tired.

"We can take Pen there," Dagger clarified. "You have to stay."

"What?" Tellus shouted.

At the same time Pen shouted, "No!"

"It's the rules." Dagger shrugged. "Any mortal who enters here dies, so they can't leave."

"You can't keep me here," Tellus pleaded.

"Rules, sorry. You're dead now."

Tellus spluttered, too shocked to reply.

Pen turned to Dagger. "Any mortal who enters here loses their soul, right? That's how they die?"

"Yes."

"But his soul didn't leave him." She turned on Scythe. "You said as much when he got here."

"Aye," she said.

Pen wouldn't let them take Tellus. "He can't die because Nyx isn't here to take his soul. He's not dead, and you said the *dead* can't leave."

Dagger and Scythe exchanged glances, not happy to be caught in their own loophole.

"One moment." They left Pen and Tellus to talk in private.

"Pen, if they don't let me leave, you have to go," Tellus said in a hushed tone.

"No. I'm not abandoning you here."

"They probably don't care either way; they just follow their precious rules."

"You're honestly okay with the thought of staying here with these ghosts?"

"Obviously not, but once you release Nyx the natural order will continue, and I'll die. I don't want to be stuck down here like a mindless shade, but *I'll* be gone even if I don't know it. And everyone above will be alright."

He was thinking of Aethra and Aegeus; he was willing to die for them, as she was for Arch and Alard.

Before Pen could reply, Dagger and Scythe returned. Neither looked pleased, but they were resigned.

"You can go," Scythe said to Tellus.

Relief replaced the fear in his eyes, and Pen could breathe again too.

"Technically, you are right," Dagger said to Pen, grimacing, "the dead can't leave, and he's not dead. Think of his return as the favor for a favor that you humans are so fond of. But don't spread the idea."

"Thank you," Pen said.

"Now," Scythe said, turning to Pen, "you need to think of the place you want to go. Picture where Nyx is and hold it in your mind. Also, take his hand since he's never been there before."

Tellus reached for Pen's hand without hesitation. She appreciated the small comfort, though she still felt cold.

"Both of you close your eyes." They did. "Pen, you think of where Nyx is. Tellus, keep your mind blank. Do not think of anything."

Pen couldn't see, but she felt Scythe's hand on her left shoulder and Tellus's hand in hers. She focused on the willow tree with the graves beneath. After months of avoiding this thought, to the point where she had completely blocked it out without realizing it, it was as if her mind wanted to turn away again. She wanted to cast the image aside like a leaf in the wind, as she had so many other times, but she steeled herself and focused on that tree. She saw the long leaves swaying.

Scythe's hand withdrew. The pressure on Pen's shoulder was gone and the air was different. She waited, but nothing else happened. Confused, she slowly opened one eye, then both snapped open. The willow tree stood before her. There had been no light or rush of air to indicate travel. They had simply appeared here, as Nyx had before.

The willow had shed its leaves for the season, but the long branches still hung like a veil. The ground had frosted and become hard, but no snow had fallen yet. At the base of the trunk among the roots were two graves, one large and one small.

Tellus released her hand. "You said Nyx is buried between them?"

"Yes." The air was cleaner here, fresher, and the near winter chill did nothing for her already trembling nerves. That goddess would not be happy once released.

"Do you have a shovel?"

"Yes, yes." She forced her feet to move. The cabin they had lived in was behind her. It looked the same as ever, as if the coming winter had frozen everything in place. She spotted the shovel on the ground with the other various tools; at least that was a small change. Arch usually set them so they were standing against the house. It felt like mere seconds had passed since their deaths.

Pen went and grabbed the shovel, but then approaching the graves felt like moving through thickening smoke. She stopped at the foot of Arch's grave, then turned to stare at Alard's. There was no mound marking Nyx's box; it was too small.

Tellus appeared beside Pen and took the shovel. He didn't say anything, only nodded. Pen pointed to where the box was buried, and Tellus started digging. It wasn't deep, and after three quick strokes he knelt and brushed dirt off from the pine box. He stood with it in his hand and came over to Pen; she had backed away from the graves.

"Do you have a crowbar?" he asked.

Pen shook her head.

Tellus shrugged and placed the box on the ground. Taking a step back, he swung the shovel overhead and brought it down hard on the wood. The pine shattered easily.

Black smoke erupted outward from the broken wood and into the crisp gray day. Smoke filled Pen's vision as she was thrown back. She struck the side of the cabin and fell. She regained her breath, clutching the back of her head. Her hand came away bloody. She was about to yell for Tellus, but she spotted him rising to his feet several yards away.

Before them, among the ruins of the little coffin, stood Nyx. Her black and white eyes bored into Pen with burning hatred.

She threw a hand up toward Pen, and Pen was pinned to the wall, hardly able to breathe from the unseen force.

Nyx stalked forward with her bone raised.

"No, wait!" Tellus lunged at Nyx to stop her.

Nyx snapped her gaze to him. Using her other arm, without touching him, she threw him. He flew through the air and crashed into the willow.

Pen yelled. Thankfully, Tellus seemed uninjured; he regained his feet and drew his sword. Pen had to act while Nyx was distracted. If she managed to calm the angry goddess, they could talk.

Drawing her blood from the back of her head, she created her own sword in her hand. As Nyx turned on Tellus, Pen felt her invisible bonds loosen.

Nyx struck at Tellus with her bone like it was a sword. He blocked her swing and avoided the contact. One graze of the bone was all Nyx needed. She darted around him, enjoying the chase. Tellus narrowly avoided her again, but he wasn't used to fighting someone so small.

Pen rushed forward and broke the bonds Nyx had set. She ran to the two and swung at Nyx, aiming to incapacitate her. She had no idea if the goddess could sleep or be knocked out, but it was worth a try.

Tellus gave Pen away; she saw his eyes dart to her then back to Nyx. It was all Nyx needed. She blocked Pen's crimson blade with her bone, redirected the attack, and nearly knocked her off her feet. Pen felt the slight rush of air as the bone almost grazed her ankle.

Pen sidestepped, gaining distance and distracting Nyx from Tellus, who was circling around Nyx, trying to flank her.

"We're here to let you go," Pen stated, half panicked. "There's no need to fight."

"No need!" Nyx screamed in her adult voice. "You locked me away for months, and you just want to say 'sorry'? I was conscious the entire time, and I could feel every soul call out for me. I could feel their pain and do nothing!"

Nyx struck at Pen. Pen wasn't used to fighting with a small opponent either, but she managed to block the bone with her sword. The shock vibrated down the blade and shook her arm. Pen held her stance against Nyx's fury. She drew blood from the back of her head again. The new tendril started to fall behind her back, gaining thickness at the end, like an odd raindrop. Concentrating on the new ball, Pen swung it around and struck Nyx in the chest.

Nyx was thrown back toward the house. She managed to keep the bone in hand, but she was on her back.

Tellus rushed to her while she was stunned. Stepping on her arm that held the bone, he angled his sword at her throat.

"Your anger is justified," he said, "but there is no need to fight."

"My quarrel is not with you," Nyx growled.

"Then stop this!"

Nyx flung her other hand up, and Tellus flew off her. There was enough force this time to send him smashing into the willow. Pen heard a sickening crunch, and Tellus lay still on the ground.

The sword wasn't enough. Putting herself between Nyx and Tellus, Pen changed her weapon into a long spear. Nyx rushed at her, Pen parried the bone and stabbed, but Nyx evaded the blade. Nyx dashed around Pen and attacked from the right side. Pen went to block, but it was a bluff.

Nyx darted left and would have broken Pen's leg if Pen hadn't used the back of the spear to parry the bone. She raised the weapon to bash Nyx on the temple, but Nyx danced away.

Pen spun with the goddess, changing her weapon again. A spear was no good in close combat. She now held a thick axe blade, but Nyx blocked it inches from her own skull.

The goddess's black and white eyes were fuming, but Pen repressed the shudder that threatened to loosen her grip.

"I don't care if you're the bloody descendent of Maniodes," Nyx hissed. "The Blood Warrior line ends here."

"What?" Why would she mention the god of Skiachora? Come to think of it, why hadn't he been there? What did Dagger and Scythe do to him?

Nyx shoved away Pen's axe and pushed her back with invisible force, pushing Pen in the gut and ripping all air from her lungs. She fell, gasping at what felt like shards of glass in her throat. She forced herself to rise to her feet, only then realizing that her axe had melted. Blood painted the grass beside her; some of it stained Alard's grave.

Losing that blood left her shaken and drawing more would only make it worse. She drew more anyway as Nyx advanced. She considered a whip to keep the goddess at a distance, but it could get caught. She decided on two short daggers.

Nyx advanced, keeping the bone low. Pen stood her ground, not wanting to rush into the attack, given that she was already dizzy.

Tellus appeared behind Nyx, Pen hadn't seen him stand, and he grabbed Nyx's arm, pinning the bone to her side like a parent disciplining his child. His blade now angled at her throat from behind.

"Drop the bone." All desire for a parley was gone.

"You know if you cut my throat, nothing will happen," Nyx said.

"Let me prove that for myself."

Nyx spun along the blade. The metal didn't pierce her skin. She broke Tellus's grip in the surprise and swung for his head. Tellus stepped back, nearly falling, but avoided the bone by a hair.

"Leave him alone!" Pen yelled. "Your fight is with me."

Hoping that had provided a distraction, Pen darted forward, aiming at Nyx's eyes, a likely soft spot. Nyx blocked her attack and another from Tellus.

In her fury Nyx leapt higher than any mortal could, straight into the branches of the willow, and disappeared. Pen scanned the branches, sword in hand, quickly leaving the veil of hanging leaves. Tellus did the same, staying close by but checking behind them, knowing his parameters, ever the general.

One distraction was all it took. Pen and Tellus exchanged glances, and Pen was going to suggest they try to run, when she saw Nyx. She appeared behind Tellus and touched her bone to his neck.

"No!" Pen's blood dissolved, along with her will.

Tellus stood frozen, watching Pen, then he saw the bone out of the corner of his eye. The light in his eyes disappeared when Nyx removed the bone.

Tellus dropped.

Pen screamed again as she caught his body. His sword fell from his numb fingers, and she lowered him to the ground. She couldn't see through her tears. She couldn't breathe, couldn't move, and didn't want to. Tellus was dead.

Pen whipped the tears away, looking up to Nyx's childlike form. The goddess stood glaring but not attacking.

"Go on then," Pen snapped, "take me too."

"No," Nyx growled. "I said I'd punish you for locking me away, and I intend to. You will live, Pen. No matter what you endure, you will live."

And then Nyx was gone.

Chapter Seventeen

The snow was falling heavily and stood several feet high by the time Pen reached the Ragged Wolves' cavern. There was no proper doorway, but sentries met her outside, one she didn't recognize, but the other was bald Palrig. He vouched for her and sent his partner to inform Raisa.

Palrig led Pen to the central chamber with the fire pit where she had originally met them.

"So how's Tellus?" he asked.

Pen didn't reply; she only watched the fire.

Palrig must have read her emotion, because he didn't ask further.

When Raisa arrived, she dismissed Palrig and sat by the fire with Pen.

Before Raisa could say more than a greeting Pen asked, "What news from Stymphalia? Is Queen Aethra safe?"

"She's fine; I got there in time to stop the murder. She also gave birth some weeks ago. It's a healthy boy, Prince Aegeus the Second. Suppose I should say king now, though he's only a few days old."

"King Aegeus is dead?"

"Yes, from what I've gathered it was around the same time. Aethra is still queen, so she will rule until her son comes of age. I haven't heard much from Kalymnos."

"Who was the assassin, anyway? Did someone help him?"

"It was a man I knew, but he's not important. It was Tellus's second in command, actually, Connin, who helped him. Turns out his father died fighting for Kalymnos in the Ichorian War. What about you and Tellus, though? Did you find Taiphus? Something must have happened, because about a week ago Narciso passed away from his wounds; he just drifted off in his sleep. The heads we kept are finally rotting properly too."

At first Pen didn't know what Raisa meant about Taiphus, and then she remembered their lie. Pen saw no point in holding back now, so she told Raisa everything. She started with the cannibals in the forest and ended with releasing Nyx. She did, however, conceal the fact that Pen herself locked the goddess away; she covered by saying that Dagger and Scythe knew where she was, but they couldn't leave Skiachora themselves.

Raisa didn't reply for a long time. Pen stayed quiet, watching the flames; it was a lot to take in.

"What did you do with Tellus's body?" Raisa asked.

"I stole a horse from a nearby ranch and used my magic to lift him onto it and then took him back to Stymphalia. He loved that city, and his loved ones needed to know what happened to him. It took a couple of days, but I left him at the front gate at night and waited for him to be found. The guards on duty found him at dawn and carried his body inside on shields. I returned the horse once I was done, then walked here."

"Well, that explains how exhausted you look," Raisa said.

The tears escaped then, though she refused to sob and wail. She stared at the fire.

Raisa let her stay for a couple days in an empty bunk. During breakfast on the third day Pen said she was leaving.

"You can have one of our horses, we don't have much, but we'll get by without one," Raisa offered at the table in the warm kitchen. "And it seems like a poor thank you for returning the peace of death to us all."

"No, I want to go on foot," Pen said. She didn't want to grow attached to any living creature for a long while.

"But it's the dead of winter."

"I'll be fine."

Pen watched the snow fall and melt around her fire by the sheltering cliff face. She'd found an overhang to wait out the night as the moon reached its climax, the first moon of the new year.

"I always loved winter; it's cold and unforgiving, but beautiful."

Pen's heart seized as she sprang from the rock she had been sitting on, knife in hand. Scythe stood beside the fire. The blade of the tall scythe the goddess carried was hooked over her head, extending several feet above her. Scythe smiled warmly.

Pen lowered her knife but kept her grip on it; she didn't sense danger any longer, but she wasn't foolish.

"What do you want?" she demanded.

"Relax," Scythe said. "I'm here to fix what Nyx caused. Well, sort of."

"What?"

"We know what Nyx did to punish you, and I can't reverse it. She said you would live, and she meant it. She meant live forever."

Pen didn't know how to process what Scythe had just said, even though she had *seen* the impossible over the past few months.

"So... no matter what I do I can't die? At all?" Rephrasing it helped a little.

"Exactly. Nyx will never release you from the pain of living, so you can never join your loved ones. It seems amazing, but immortality does get dull now and then."

"So are you here to gloat?" she scoffed. Scythe seemed like a kind person at first, if odd, but she didn't seem like the bragging type. Pen may have kidnapped her friend but she freed the goddess. This was unnecessary and cruel.

"No," Scythe said, appearing insulted. "I told you before I'm here to help."

"But you said you can't remove Nyx's curse."

"I can't do that specifically. Once a god grants a gift or curse, it can't be taken away by another. It's another rule, so we don't constantly torment you mortals."

"Because one curse is bad enough," Pen said flatly.

"Basically, yes," Scythe said, seeming to perk up. "I can't remove Nyx's curse, but I can add to it. She made it so you will never die, but that doesn't mean you aren't aging. I can freeze you in time so you will stay as you are now."

Pen didn't reply, trying to comprehend the strange idea.

Scythe continued, "You do not want to reach two hundred years of age, unable to see or move without breaking one bone or another."

She had a point; Pen didn't want any of this, but it was too late now. She might as well take what she could while the goddess was offering.

Then a thought struck her. "Why are you offering me this?"

"While I was angry that you kidnapped my friend, you did it out of grief, with a broken mind. You then fixed the problem by releasing her right away," Scythe explained. "And I'm sorry you lost Tellus."

Pen's heart seized again. She remembered placing his sword in his cold hands when she left him by the city. She was honestly surprised by how much she missed him. They had only traveled together for a month or so, but the pain she felt was familiar. It was the same kind of hurt when she lost Arch.

"You can live for their sake, and old age is not kind when you reach the centuries," Scythe said kindly.

Pen forced a breath and said, "Alright."

She could barely live with the guilt and pain, but she could control the physical pain.

"Then it's done." Scythe nodded.

Pen didn't feel any different. "That's it?"

Scythe shrugged. "Yes, you've seen how we work. It's not *always* flashy."

Pen scoffed and nearly laughed. She couldn't think of a comeback to say to Scythe. She felt mostly numb inside. Scythe didn't seem to mind.

"What will you do now?" Scythe asked.

"I have no idea," Pen replied honestly.

Scythe shrugged again. "Fair enough. Life is more fun that way."

Pen didn't always think so, but Scythe took her leave before she could reply.

Pen sheathed her knife and settled back by the fire in her furs, content to wait out the winter, she had little choice.

Acknowledgments

I'm bad at these parts, but I'd like to thank Krista Witinko, the best co worker and friend that would listen to me rant about nonsense. My parents, Deanna and Wayne, for being awesome and supportive. And to the (figurative) voices in my head that don't shut up.

About the Author

Emilie Knight is constantly writing, and after years of reading fantasy and horror she combines them together into her own dark fantasy writing. Using her BA in Classical Civilizations and fascination in Ancient Greek mythology she blends it well into her fiction. Other then reading in her spare time she plays video games quiet often.

www.emilieknight.com

Read the first chapter of the prequel story: Dagger and Scythe

Maniodes stood in front of the fireplace in his office chambers, facing Scythe and Dagger. The fireplace was beautifully crafted from black marble, not showing a single seam. The rest of the furniture looked archaic in comparison. A single large desk and chair, both made of wrought iron and littered with parchment and quills, stood in the corner. In another corner a bench that would have been comfortable if it hadn't been made of the same iron sat. That bench was not meant for pleasant exchanges.

The short crop of his dark-blue hair glinted when the firelight hit it. It had been styled differently yesterday. Scythe knew even gods had their vanities, and she wanted to compliment him on the change, but his demeanor was overwhelming. He stood a towering eight feet as he studied Dagger and Scythe. He wasn't just angry this time; he was livid at the chaos they had caused. Scythe stayed quiet while staring at the ash on Maniodes's boots.

Beside her, Dagger was equally quiet.

Maniodes sighed, seeming to be frustrated by his own train of thought. "You were given one victim of your choice, but you decided to torch the entire village. It will be a wondrous story, true, but you left a child alive! The Incruentus Ferrum are supposed to be subtle."

His voice scared the warmth from the fire, or so it seemed to Scythe.

"It was not intended, sire," Dagger said. "We got…carried away."

Scythe had to bite her cheek to stop from laughing. She could still see Dagger stalking around the pile of bodies in the main square, relishing his work.

"Something funny, Scythe?" Maniodes asked, turning on her.

She had stifled the laugh but not the smile. She swallowed her nerves and looked up at the god. There wasn't any point in lying now.

"We got excited," she explained.

"Of course you did; that's the problem. First, you ransack that wedding, leaving no survivors. Then you, Dagger, kill a king on his ship and everyone saw you. It doesn't matter if panic ensues. You *have* to stay hidden. You are meant to cause mischief that the living can't explain, not mayhem and chaos they can fight against. Keeping them cautious keeps them safe, and it reminds them there is a higher power."

"What's the point in causing mischief if we can't enjoy it?" Dagger questioned. "And what's the point, anyway? The living cause enough chaos with war and murder. Whatever we do, it's a small percentage of what they do to themselves."

"The purpose is to be subtle and cause terror. What's more threatening—the hunter with the axe that you can see, or the monster in the shadows that stalks you? And the *point* is to frighten them in ways they can't explain easily."

Dagger didn't reply; Scythe remained quiet as well. They were lucky they could discuss things with their ruler at all, but even they knew when to shut up.

"I have an idea," Maniodes said.

Scythe hoped it didn't involve being trapped in the river Acheron again.

"You two will marry each other."

"What?!" Dagger exclaimed.

Scythe's breath locked in her chest. She had finally gained freedom in death, and now she was going to be bound to a man nonetheless.

"That's ridiculous," Dagger said, gingerly overstepping his bounds.

"You two have worked together before, regardless of my say-so. And that's more than most mortals get in arranged marriages," Maniodes said civilly.

"But a marriage as a punishment?" Dagger asked.

"Call it an experiment. Conventional punishments haven't worked on either of you, and I don't want to rip away your lives. You two will guard each other. If one of you takes a step out of bounds, then both of you will go grey and rejoin the dead in the fields."

"Guarding each other I understand, even forcing us to live together, but why the full marriage?" Dagger asked again.

"God of mischief," Maniodes shrugged. "You two work well together anyway. Forcing the marriage should remind you who is in charge."

Scythe stared at Maniodes, the insult tasting bitter. They'd had a silent understanding of her rogue behavior so long as she followed the basic rules. Forcing this upon her was almost as bad as what her father had tried to pull.

Maniodes turned to Scythe. She didn't bother hiding her anger. He knew her story. It was why he chose her to become an Incruentus Ferrum. He guarded his expression well. She couldn't tell if he was saddened by her rage, emboldened by his victory, or if he even gave a shit.

"Come, stand here." Maniodes indicated for them to move closer.

Dagger stepped forward, but Scythe stayed put, nails biting into her palms.

"Scythe."

The cold tone of a father talking down to a child, while also threatening to kill that child, compelled her to move. She hated herself and Maniodes for it, but she couldn't become one of those mindless, stumbling shades. She took her place beside Dagger but couldn't look at him.

"Raise your left hand," Maniodes ordered.

Scythe did so and held it palm-down just over waist height.

"Dagger, your right."

Dagger raised his hand and held Scythe's from below. Their fingers wove together naturally. She forced herself to not let go. Dagger hadn't wanted this, either. He'd even protested against it.

"Shit, I don't have a ribbon," Maniodes admitted, looking at their joined hands. "Hold on."

He unclipped a chain hanging from his belt. Using that instead of the customary ribbon, the god laid it over Scythe's hand, wrapped it under Dagger's, then over again.

Once the chain encircled their wrists Maniodes spoke again.

"I won't bother with fancy words. Dagger, do you take this woman as your wife?"

Dagger cleared his throat, then said, "Yes."

"Scythe, do you take this man as your husband?"

If she said no she'd be dead. Swallowing her pride, she said, "Yes."

"Good. Now, if either of you disobey my order again, I will strip the consciousness from you both. You are to watch and guide each other. Understood?"

"Yes," Dagger said.

Scythe nodded.

"Should things go well and you learn to control ourselves, I could grant an annulment," Maniodes said. "Now go. I don't care where, neither of you will receive any work for a while."

Made in the USA
Coppell, TX
23 March 2022